Nickolas

THE GRANT BROTHERS SERIES BOOK 1

KATHI S. BARTON

World Castle Publishing
Pensacola, Florida
Copyright © by Kathi S. Barton 2011
Paperback ISBN: 9781937085216
eBook ISBN: 9781937085421
Library of Congress Catalogue Number 2011928101
First Edition World Castle Publishing June 15, 2011
http://www.worldcastlepublishing.com
License Notes
Cover Artist: Fantasia Frogs Design
Editor: Brieanna Robertson

DEDICATION

To my very best friend and the biggest nag I know, Charlotte Blackwell. Thank you for pushing me to write these for you and keeping me on my toes with your help and comments. I love you very much, Kiddo.

CHAPTER ONE

Nick looked across his desk at the young woman applying for the position. *Okay, I must have heard her wrong. There's no way she just said what I think she said. I'm just tired. I've conducted at least twenty of these interviews today and I'm just a little punch drunk. Hiring a receptionist/secretary is not as easy as I thought. Let's try this again.*

"You came here today for this interview, why, again?" Same question really, just a bit more...specific.

"I said my parole officer said I had to come. She said that I needed to make 'amends,' or some other crap. I don't know. Look, Randall didn't take anything from you, so I don't know why she said I had to come here precisely. I told her I thought it was a bad idea, but she was insistent."

He just stared. *Okay. Take. She said she did not take anything from him. A thief. Why on earth would I want to hire a thief?*

"I haven't the foggiest idea either. Ms. Morgan, I think this is a mistake. Maybe my brothers know your, ummm...parole officer and set this up as a joke of some sort."

Nickolas was going to kill Damon. This sounded just like something he would do. He gathered up Becky Morgan's file and closed it. He stood up to walk her to the door to his office, but got no further than just standing up. He'd toss it in the trash after she left. She stood up, too, and pulled down her mini-skirt again. She had done that several times already. Well, he would give her points for that; she was not stupid enough to believe he would hire her just because she had a nice set of shapely legs and a pretty face.

Her eyes were a shade of blue he had never seen before, almost silver. Her hair hung in a fat braid down her back. Wisps of it curled around her face and slim neck, making her swipe at it annoyingly. Her lips were full and kissable, without a trace of gloss or lipstick. Freckles danced across her nose and along her high cheekbones. She was tall, probably five-ten in her bare feet. She'd just fit under his chin if he were to stand next to her. Her breasts were full, if the view from where he was sitting was any indication. Nick shook his head. *What am I thinking? Focus here, idiot. On her, not her body, damn it.*

"Yeah, could be. Well, you'll tell Ms. Parker that I came by before you throw out my application, won't you? Yeah, I can see you eyeing the circular filing cabinet. She said to have you call her, that you'd know the number and all."

"Margaret Parker? Margaret Parker is your parole officer?" He sat back down, harder than he expected, and clipped his tongue with his teeth coming together. *Shit!*

"Yeah, she said you knew her or some other sh...stuff. You okay? You look sort of...well, I was gonna say stiff, but that's probably not possible. You already look like a rod has replaced your spine." She was glaring at him.

His mother. His mother sent him a thief as a potential employee. He opened her file again and really looked at it. He was going to ignore the reference to his spine and the rod; his brothers had been saying something similar to that to him for the past six months. Then he leaned back in his chair and began to massage his forehead right between his eyes. Why did the tension always start there? There was an annoyance in the middle of his chest too.

Okay, let's get to the bottom of this. He sat upright again and forced himself to focus on the task at hand. "This is an investment firm, Ms. Morgan. We handle other people's money, a lot of money, every day. Tell me what you stole and why?" He wanted to get to the bottom of this quickly so he could truthfully tell his mother that he had interviewed Ms. Morgan, but wouldn't be able to hire her.

He looked up at her when he didn't hear anything from her for a few seconds.

"I didn't steal anything. Randall did. I wasn't even convicted. At least not of that—I didn't even know that was going on. I didn't go to jail for that anyway. I went to jail for murder, Mr. Pompous Ass."

Murder? Pompous ass? Whoa!

"Hold on a minute. You went to jail for *murder*?"

"Yeah, but not for long. They let me off. I was ... I can't remember what it's called, but they figured out I was telling the truth and that it was self-defense. He deserved to die." Her voice was hard; he could hear the barely controlled anger.

"Who deserved to die?" Nick's head was spinning with all this information. Die? Self-defense? What the...?

"Some guy. It's none of your business since you've already decided I'm not good enough for your precious firm."

He watched as she leaned over and picked up her bag, and he got a very nice view down her blouse. Oh yeah, those were very nice and full. Her bag, the thing was really too big to call a purse, was slung over her shoulder as she stood back up. She was halfway to the door when he cleared his throat.

"Are you leaving? Now? I thought you said that you had to come here for this?" He stood, moved to the other side of his desk, and leaned against it. His headache was now thrumming through his body, making him slightly sick to his stomach.

She stood by the door, her hand on the knob and her back to him. Even from across the room, he could see that she was trembling. From what, he wasn't sure; anger came to mind first, but why was she mad, he didn't know. He'd been the one who had been tricked into this mess.

"Yes. Yes, I'm leaving now. I'm leaving before I say something I'll regret. Maybe I'll regret, I don't know. Maybe I won't regret it until tomorrow or the next day, if ever, you ... you stupid jerk. Have a good day, Mr. Investment Banker Grant." She opened the door without a backward glance and closed it quietly behind her.

Nick sat there for a good two minutes without a thought in his head and stared at the door she'd just left through. Then he jumped up and called the lobby. He knew he'd be cutting it close, but he wasn't going to let her get away with that last comment. Jerk indeed.

"David, its Nick Grant. There's a young woman coming down. I need you to detain her. Hummm...nice body, she has a head of dark red hair, a short skirt, huge pink bag. Tell her I'll be down momentarily." He hung up, confident in David Tulle's ability as his security guard to keep her there until he made another phone call.

"Mom, it's Nick, your son. Want to explain to me why you sent me an ex-con to interview?" He was moving toward the stairs, knowing that if he took the elevator, he'd lose the connection with her. And he wanted to hear her reasons before he talked with Ms. Morgan again.

CHAPTER TWO

"Nicky, love, I know it's you. They've invented this new thing called caller ID, perhaps you've heard of it. It puts your name right there on the phone for me to see, along with your phone number. And what ex-con did I send you? Because I do believe I'd remember even that in my dotage."

It was a good thing he loved her, he thought, or he'd seriously have to consider parenticide.

"Becky Morgan. And don't try to deny it, because she told me that you told me to call you when she left." He had to stop on the stairs and catch his breath. He ran eighteen miles a day on the treadmill. What was wrong with him? he wondered.

"First of all, her name is not Becky Morgan. Don't you read anything anymore? Secondly...hang on; I have to take this call."

He pulled the phone from his ear and looked at it. She put him on hold! He started walking down the steps again, a little slower. Just three more flights to go. After five minutes, she came back on the line.

"Nicky, darling, did you have that poor man David try to detain your so called ex-con?"

He was almost afraid to answer that. He could hear that tone in her voice, the *Mom* tone. It said, "Don't even try lying because I already know the truth."

"I might have. Why?" He was at the door at the lobby now, but didn't go through it. If he had to grovel to his mom, he was *not* going to let everyone in the lobby hear it.

"Well, they've just called the paramedics for him. He is bleeding on the ugly carpet I told you not to put in. It's much too sedate and boring. You should have gone with the royal blue one—"

"Mom! I need you to focus here. Why are the paramedics on their way for David?" He pushed the door open with a bang. He was three feet from a crowd gathered around what he could only assume was his security guard.

"She said that she asked him several times not to touch her, and she also warned him that she could and would defend herself if he did. She said that he grabbed her arm and ripped her shirt—a borrowed shirt I might add. What is wrong with you? Are you actually telling your employees to accost young women now? Nicholas Patrick Grant, I'm very angry with you right now." He could hear it too.

Nickolas could hear her voice get just a tad more pitch behind it with every word until she got to his full name. A kid always knew when he was in trouble because his mom would use his entire name to yell for him. It didn't change much as an adult either.

"Are you saying that Becky attacked David? That just doesn't sound—"

"Her name is Morgan Becky, not Becky Morgan, you jackass. And why would I lie to you, I ask you? I sent her in there in good faith to get a job. And what do you do? You—"

"Mom she's an ex-con, I can't—"

"You will not interrupt your mother again, young man. She is *not* an ex-con. She was acquitted of all charges and released.

I am not her parole officer; I'm her counselor and friend. Well, probably not after this. How could you?"

He could hear the hurt in her voice and felt bad that he had put it there.

Nickolas didn't know what to say. He felt like he was six years old again and had just broken the cookie jar. Or rather, his brother Jamie had broken it—he'd just dared him to it. Of course ,Jamie had done it; he never could turn down a dare.

"Mom, I'm sorry. Let me see to David, and then I'll find Ms. Mor ... Becky, and make it up to her. I'm really sorry."

"See that you do. And I want you to call me as soon as you have apologized to her. Apologized to her several times, I mean. Nickolas, if you don't make this right, I'll go back to setting you up with potential wives again. I swear. And I won't be as choosy this time."

"God, no! Please don't do that. I beg you, please. I'll make it up to her, I swear. You can depend on me." That was a promise he would follow through on even if he had to buy the little twit all of Tiffany's.to make her happy.

Nick walked over to the scene and, in a glance, could see that David was indeed in need of paramedics. His head was bleeding quite profusely from the open wound on the back. One of the girls from his brother Damon's office—he had an office in the building too—was holding a pad over it and talking quietly to him. And there stood Ms. Mor ... Becky, nearly vibrating in her anger.

"You all right, David? Did anyone call your wife?" He decided to ignore the beautiful woman for now, at least until he got a better control on his temper.

"Yes, sir. Roger called her. She's gonna meet me there. It's all my fault, Mr. Grant. Miss Becky told me to let her go and she said that she'd hurt me if I didn't. I should have just let her go like she said. My missus is gonna be pissed about this. I ripped her shirt too. Miss Becky's, I mean." David handed the small strip of material over to Nick that he still had clutched in his hand. Nick looked up at Morgan.

"Don't you have something to say to David, Ms. Becky? I mean, was it really necessary to hit him in the head?" Her hands were trembling when she took the material from him. Snatched would have been a better word, but he let it go. He was in enough trouble with his mother without adding insult to injury.

"You mean I should apologize? I don't think so. I'm sorry he was hurt. I never meant for him to hit his head. If anyone should apologize, it should be you."

"Me? What the hell did I do? You're the one who knocked him over. I wasn't finished talking to you and you left."

"Screw you." And with that, she turned on her heel and stormed out of the building. Nick would have given chase, but the ambulance showed up just then and, as David's employer, he felt it was his duty to go with him.

David Tulle was fine after a quick trip to the hospital and fifteen stitches later. When he had grabbed at Morgan's arm as she moved to pass him, she countered with a sweep of her leg under his and threw him to the floor. Falling down, he had hit his head on the corner of the front desk, grabbing at her borrowed shirt and ripping it.

Of course, the firm paid for the entire thing and even sprang for lunch for David and his obviously pregnant wife, who had met them at the hospital. Nick then made the trip back to the office to pick up Ms. Becky's file and make everything all right with his mom. No way was he letting her set him up on blind dates again.

Nick was okay with being single. He dated when he wanted to, which wasn't really that often. At twenty-nine, he was a widower of nearly eight years now.

His wife Nancy had been killed in a car crash about a year into their marriage, along with his dad on their way back from dropping him off at the airport. He had been on his way to a conference in Milan when slick roads and a drunk driver had crashed into them.

CHAPTER THREE

Finding Ms. Becky proved to be much harder than he had thought it would be. The cell phone number she had listed belonged to the group home she was staying in. The warden, because there was no way he was calling her Betty White, had told him in a stern voice that her clients were not allowed to have the phones for more than one trip out of the house, and they had to return them to her or else. He didn't ask what the "or else" constituted; no way did he want to know. When he asked to leave a message, the warden said she was *not* her secretary, so no; she would *not* take a message for Ms. Becky.

He drove there next. As he got close, he really wished he hadn't. The neighborhood was one that he would never be caught in after dark—maybe even after the sun came up, either. The building had been a grade school at one time, he guessed, and was now a halfway house for female ex-cons. He was given a pager and told to wait in the main hall. If Morgan wanted to see him, she'd page him and then someone would take him to her.

As he sat there waiting in the foyer, one tough-looking woman after another passed him, eyeing him up and down appreciatively. *Is my shirttail out or what?* he wondered. There was a full-length mirror in the hallway, so he surreptitiously checked himself out.

He had always considered himself an okay-looking guy. He was tall, six-five in his stocking feet. His hair was black, so black it had a blue sheen to it, and straight as a poker, as his Dad used to say. He had a nice eight-pack that he worked very hard to maintain with exercise and healthy eating. His eyes were perhaps his best feature, he thought — light gray, almost a clear blue in the sunlight. But right now, at this moment, he felt like a slab of meat hanging on a rack somewhere.

As word got around that someone had a male visitor sitting in the entrance hallway, more women found a reason to pass by and gawk at him. The women, and he wasn't always sure about that, came out in droves to stare at him. One woman had even asked him to turn around so she could see his "nice ass." He felt really stupid, but did turn around for her, but it was mostly to have her stop staring at his crotch. She hooted with laughter and made rude sucking noises to her friends.

He took out his cell phone and called his mom again. If ever a guy needed his mommy, it was now.

"Mom, it's Nick, your son. Have you ever been down here where Ms. Becky is staying?" He had kept his voice low — there wasn't any sense in offending anyone.

"No, why? I heard once it was a big place, but not much more. It's sort of a revolving door for most of them. They have to stay there until they have a permanent place to live. Most of them end up back in the same situation as they were when they got into trouble."

"It's in a questionable neighborhood. Actually, I would consider that to be an understatement. It's in a horrible part of t — "

Suddenly, he was interrupted by a loud voice. "Hey, ass boy!! Turn around; let me see your stuff. I need a man, and you look like you can handle a woman like me." He looked around and saw a huge, voluptuous African–American woman staring at him lasciviously.

"Uh, Mom—"

"Leave the building right now, Nick. Turn around and get out." He decided his mother's advice was right on for a change. He got up and started to leave.

"Where you going? Come on back here. I want some lovin' and you're gonna do it. I don't wanna have to hurt you." He glanced back once and saw that she was lumbering toward him. He took another hasty step forward and felt someone grab his arm. He was being jerked around before he could he could blink.

"Whoa!"

"Nickolas, get out! Right now!"

He tried, he really did. The huge momma pressed herself against him and tried to kiss him. As he was trying to extricate himself, he heard another voice, one he was vaguely familiar with.

"Big Martha, you need to step away from that man. He's here to see me. Why, I have no idea, but I'm sure he'll tell me. I don't want to have to hurt you, so step away." Morgan Becky. He couldn't see her around the woman who was now groping his crotch.

"You? A little thing like you? Get real. I ain't afraid of a little nothing like you." She banged his head against the wall as she spoke.

Nick was starting to get a headache again. *Wham!* Suddenly everything went black.

~~~

"Oh, don't be ridiculous, Morgan. Of course not. You have to be able to get there first, don't you? Why you are so stubborn is beyond me." Nick woke up to the sound of his mother's voice, then he heard her huff. He'd never heard his mother huff at anyone but him and his brothers before and wondered at the cause.

He opened his eyes, and looked around. He was obviously in a hospital room, but why? Thinking hurt his head. He tried to move his hand up to touch his forehead, but he ended up hitting himself in the head with the board attached to his wrist with the IV in it.

"Mom? What happened? Why am I in the hospital?" He moved to sit up straighter and got a stabbing pain in his right temple for his effort. He had to take a couple of deep breaths and close his eyes before he moved again.

He heard another voice. "I hit you. It wasn't on purpose. You sort of got used as a human shield and your eye got in the way. The doc said you'd be okay in the morning, only a little bruising." He looked over and saw the ex-con, or whatever she was. *What's her name again? Morgan.* Her lip was swollen and her jaw had a large bruise on it. He also noticed that she had a tear in her T-shirt. *My eye got in the way? Huh?*

"Oh, Nicky. I told you to leave. Why the hell didn't you listen to me? You aren't used to those kinds of women and she could have really hurt you." His mother didn't sound very motherly at the moment, but pissed off.

"I'm in the hospital. I think someone did hurt me." He turned to Morgan. "Who did that to you? What did you call her? Big Martha?"

Instead of answering, Morgan pursed her lips, stood up, opened the curtain that surrounded the bed, and walked away. ER. He was still in the emergency room.

"She really didn't mean to hurt you, you know. She told the

police that she was trying to rescue you from Big Martha, and when Martha pulled you in front of her, she couldn't stop her foot from connecting with your face. She won't let anyone look at her, but the woman who runs the place, Ms. White, said that she took quite a beating from Martha's crew before she rendered Martha unconscious."

She knocked Big Martha out? While she was outnumbered? He didn't remember that, or anything else, as a matter of fact, after Big Martha went after him.

"Did she say *why* she won't let anyone look at her?" Things were starting to come back now with alarming clarity. That big woman, presumably Big Martha, had said she needed some loving. And he was going to give it to her. He shuddered at that. He remembered Morgan's voice and she had asked her to let him go, that he'd come to see her.

"She won't say, stubborn girl. Why I'd like to tan both —"

Just then, the doctor walked in.

"Hello, Mr. Grant. How are you this fine morning? Quite a beating you took there. Let's have a look at those peepers, why don't we? Ms. Parker, how are you?" Dr. Emily Fraley took out her little flashlight and pointed it at his left eye. The pain was immediate and sharp and he jerked back from it. She let him, and then frowned down at him.

That couldn't be good, he thought. "What? You frowned." He rubbed his chest. There was that annoyance again. He refused to call it a pain.

"I'm going to want to keep you overnight. I don't like what I see in your eyes. I think you might have a good-sized concussion." She took his chart off the end of his bed and made some notes.

How could I have any-sized concussion from a foot to the head? And how the hell did she get her foot that far up? I'm six–five! And where the hell did the owner of that foot go, anyway?

"Where did Ms. Becky go, Mom? She should have to stay too. She's the one who kicked me." He believed in equal punishment for equal guilt.

"The young woman? Oh, that policeman, Officer Denty, is still talking to her. She's just down the hall, I think. Mr. Grant, is there someone who could bring you some personal things? I'll see where we can put you now." Dr. Fraley disappeared around the curtain, his mom close on her heels. He hoped Mom was going to see to Morgan. The silly girl needed to be looked at too.

CHAPTER FOUR

"Are you paying attention to me, girly? I don't think you're givin' me the respect this here badge says you should." Officer Alex Denty had been talking at her for the past twenty minutes. This was the second time he'd referred to his badge like it was the Holy Grail or something. But she'd learned that you didn't argue with the badge, or the man behind it.

"Yes, sir, I'm paying attention. You said that my things at the halfway house had been destroyed. And I do respect you as an officer." She looked down the hall and saw Ms. Parker coming their way. Shit! She *so* didn't need this.

"Hello, Denty. Don't you have other innocent victims to harass? This 'girly' is with me, and you know how much respect I have for you, you ..."

Morgan started to laugh, and then quickly turned it into a cough when the cop jerked back around to her. She didn't have a lot to laugh at most of the time, so that had caught her off guard. She nearly missed the wink Ms. Parker sent her way.

"I was just tellin' the ... Ms. Morgan here that her things got torn up at the halfway house, ain't nothing left. Not that she had much anyways, but there you have it. You can't go back neither. Mrs. White says she runs a respectable place and she ain't having you causing trouble."

Morgan glanced at Ms. Parker. No hope for it, she'd heard.

"Thank you, Officer Denty. I appreciate you giving me the time out of your busy schedule to let me know." Morgan started to walk away, toward the exit, hoping she could get out before he said something else she didn't want everyone to know.

But Mrs. Parker jumped in. "Wait! Wait right there, young lady." Morgan turned when she yelled; she had been drilled on stopping when told. "Officer Denty, are you going to do anything about her things being destroyed? Destruction of property? Invasion of privacy? You know, do your job?"

The officer answered Mrs. Parker, but never took his eyes from Morgan. "There weren't nothing there really. Little bit of clothes, some books, nothing to get all twisted up about, is there, Ms. Morgan?"

It was that tone, the tone that said, *You agree with me or find yourself at the wrong end of my fist sometime in the near future.*

"Nothing worth getting upset over, Ms. Parker. Really, it's all right. I have the important stuff with me. Please, it's okay. I'm okay with this." Morgan looked at her and hoped she would just back off. She didn't need any more trouble right now.

"Morgan is her first name, not her last. Morgan, go to Nick's area and wait for me there. And I mean right there, you understand? Mr. Denty and I have a few things to discuss in private."

Morgan hesitated. She didn't want to. She didn't want to go back to the arrogant ass, nor did she want to leave this woman alone with the cop. She actually thought Ms. Parker might hurt him.

"Yes, ma'am." She moved toward the curtained area, dragging her feet as she went.

Margaret had said his area, not right at his bedside, so Morgan waited on the outside of Nickolas' curtain, pacing back and forth, muttering to herself. "I'm an adult, not a child, and I wish people would flipping remember that. What does she think I'll do, roam around the hospital and cause trouble for someone else?"

"I would say that's a yes. Trouble does seem to follow you around fairly close. I've been to this hospital more in the past twenty-four hours than I have been in the past twenty-four days," Nickolas said from the other side of the curtained area.

Morgan saw red.

Morgan flipped the curtain back so quickly that the nurse standing next to his bed jumped like she'd been struck by something. Morgan paid little attention to her and lit into the man on the bed.

"Why you arrogant, pigheaded, overbearing, egotistical prick. You have the nerve, the very nerve, to make this my fault. *Mine?* Are you seriously thinking that you had nothing to do with this entire event?

"First, you told that security guard to detain me, to keep me there until you got your stuffy ass down there to grace me with your presence. And I warned him not to touch me, but, oh no, he had to ignore that. Then you're the one who came to the halfway house to see me—I didn't invite you there. And you're the one who let himself get close enough to Big Martha to be used as a shield. It was you who ... who, oh, shit! I'm gonna be sick." She glanced quickly at the nurse now, and ran in the direction she indicated, holding one hand over her stomach and the other over her mouth.

Morgan hated getting upset, especially mad upset. She really hated getting mad and loud upset. She heaved the very little food she'd had on her belly and sat there on the floor for several minutes afterwards, just resting and thinking. *Shit! I can't go back to the halfway house. Now what the hell do I do?*

Morgan didn't have any clothes, just the ones she had on and the three or four pair of panties she always carried with her. There was also an extra T-shirt and some clean socks. The prison had given her five hundred dollars when they had let her go, and she had wisely put that in a plastic baggie in the waistband of her jeans. She still had over four hundred and fifty of that left.

Her other belongings, the ones now destroyed rubble at the house, were two books that she'd not finished reading, three more T-shirts, another pair of jeans, bras and more panties. There was also an assortment of toiletries. She'd not purchased anything else, thinking—well, hoping really—she'd be able to get a job before she needed a coat and things like that. She didn't have any family, so there were no letters from home, nor any pictures.

She was still deep in thought when someone knocked at the bathroom door.

"Morgan, are you all right?" Ms. Parker must have finished with Denty. She had really hoped that she'd just go home with her son and forget about her. No such luck.

"Yeah, I'm fine. I'm coming out in a second." She stood up and dug into the big bag and found her toothbrush and toothpaste. She took several paper towels and, after wetting them really well, she washed down the sink and the spigots with the soap in the dispenser. She wasn't a clean freak, but she was in a hospital where people were sick. She didn't want to take any chances with catching something lingering. She didn't mind dying, would probably welcome it, she mused, but she didn't want to spend the next ten years dying from something she'd caught here. After thoroughly brushing her teeth and her tongue twice, she opened the door.

CHAPTER FIVE

Nick looked up at three of his brothers. He was not amused by their presence, or their comments. Damon had come on the scene just as Morgan had started her tirade at him. He had rushed around the curtain in time to see her beat it to the bathroom to be sick. Then when Jamie and Byron had come in, Damon told them the story in great detail and with lots of embellishments.

"She did not call me a self-righteous prig. If you are going to tell the story, at least tell it without lying," Nick told Damon. "Where is she anyway? Mom said she was having issues with her and she'd be right back." He was in a room now, and his head was hurting a whole lot less now that they had given him something for the intense pain shooting from his temple to his eyeball. He rubbed his chest again, and noticed that Damon was starting at him intently.

"You gonna get that checked? Or am I gonna have to have Mom haul your ass in my office again?" Damon, the second oldest, was a doctor. He'd been a great surgeon until a few years ago, when he'd quit the hospital without a backward glance and opened his own practice in the same building as Nick owned.

"I don't know what you're talking about. I've had a really shitty day, in case you hadn't noticed." He leaned back against the bed and tried not to think about the burning in his chest.

He needed to focus on something besides the pain. He thought instead of the girl who had disrupted his otherwise...okay, boring life.

"Mom said that she doesn't know where she is and she's trying to find her. She seemed pretty upset when I saw her before I came in here. Who is this chick anyway?" Spencer said as he came in the door with his youngest brother, Devin.

Great! Just friggin great! All five of them. Could this day get any worse? Nick groaned loudly when Damon started the story over yet again, with even more elaborate details from Jamie and Byron who weren't even in the room when it happened.

"You all had better have a kiss for your poor old mother, or I'm going to get really mad." Margaret Parker always made a grand entrance. "Chick? I'll have you know she is a grown woman. And if I hear that derogatory word from your mouth again without referring to a baby chicken, I *will* wash it out with a bar of lye soap, young man. She's my friend still, no thanks to your brother. I'm trying to find her a steady job and now housing, if I can locate the little nitwit." She simply stood by the only chair in the room and Nick watched as his brother Byron nearly fell over getting up for her to sit down.

He smiled at her grouse. His mother was, by and far, the most loved mother of all time, he was sure. She had her six sons wrapped quite tightly around her little finger. And she knew it.

After the lavish compliments, hugs and kisses, they settled down on any available place they could in Nick's private room. He had had to move his legs twice to make room for two of his brothers. Devin ordered pizzas for them, plus the nursing staff, and had bribed one of the delivery people stop and get a six pack of his favorite dark beer. It helped that he owned the shop, he supposed.

They were all successful, men of worth, as their grandfather had called them. Each of them had gone to college on an academic scholarship, despite the fact that they could afford any university they wanted to go to.

Spencer and Jamie were university professors, Spencer with tenure. Devin had his own practice, and also a tenant in his building as a criminal lawyer. Damon, too, had a practice in the Grant building. Byron had an office there, as well, but was seldom in residence. He was a famous artist and potter. His staff worked from the third and fourth floors, taking orders, setting up shows and keeping track of Byron, who needed a keeper more than any kid would.

"Wait! She was staying at the halfway house where I was ... where that ... where I was hurt." He *so* did not want his brothers to find out that he had nearly been Big Martha's lover in a house of recently released prisoners. Women prisoners.

"Well, that's where she was until she had to rescue you today. Apparently, while she was here, a few of Big Martha's crew went in and tore all of her things up, and what they couldn't destroy, they set fire to. And because of the 'disruptions' she caused, she's been told she can't stay there any longer. And now ... now I can't find her." Nick felt his mother's pointed glare at him and flushed. He was rubbing his chest again before he knew it.

"When was the last time you saw her, and where?" Damon was speaking to his mother, but watching him. Nick put his hand under the blanket. Damon's penetrating stare was starting to make him uncomfortable, and before he knew it, he was back to rubbing again. Well, fuck.

"She was in the hall with that cop, Denty. I really despise that man—arrogant asshole. I sent her back to Nicky to wait so that I could give him a piece of my mind, but when I got there, she wasn't. Did either of you see her?" Nick looked at his brother when his mother asked him.

"She was with him when I got here, but took off to the ladies room seconds later. She was sick, she said. She'd been browbeating this one here and suddenly needed to throw up. That pretty nurse came in just after, and we got busy moving Nick up here. I didn't think to check on her since then. You?" Damon nodded toward him.

Nick hated to admit it, but he hadn't thought of her either. "She couldn't have gotten far. I mean, didn't you say she was beaten up, too? I still don't understand why you didn't just make her get checked out—you have no problem telling *us* what to do on a daily basis." He started to glare at her, but decided that wasn't such a smart move. He loved his mom very much, but frankly, she still frightened him a tad.

"She isn't my son, and, by far, more than a little—" She stopped when his room door was thrown open.

"Ms. Parker? That woman you were asking about? They just found her down in x-ray. Somebody knocked her out with something. They're taking her to ER now. I don't know any more than that." The obviously flustered nurse came in and took Nick's blood pressure, then *tsk, tsked* at the elevation.

After a few seconds of noisy silence, his mom slapped Damon on the arm to get him moving. "Don't just stand there. Go to ER and see to her!" And he took off.

CHAPTER SIX

Morgan suddenly popped open her eyes. It paid to be alert and ready at all times when you were in prison, and now that she was out, it wasn't any different.

The man sitting in the chair directly in front of her simply stared, not saying a word. He didn't move, but continued to look back at her. A quick glance around the room told her a couple of things. She was in a hospital room, not a cubical in the emergency room. And she was in a private room, and it was a really nice room at that.

Morgan rolled to her back and moaned at the pain that shot through her body. She closed her eyes against the onslaught of agony that raced to every nerve in her. She wondered vaguely if there was a single muscle that didn't hurt right now.

"You have a deep concussion to the left side of your head, just above your ear. I had to put in seventeen stitches to close it up. X-rays show no brain swelling, but we'll check it again in the morning with another one to be sure. You have two broken ribs, as I'm sure you felt when you rolled over like that," Damon Grant said. She looked back over at him.

Morgan didn't say anything. What was there to say? He'd put the stitches in so he was a doctor; he dressed much too nice to be a nurse. She didn't need to ask him what had happened, or who'd done it. She knew the answer to both of those questions too.

Moving her right hand over her abdomen, she felt her money missing, and that they had not catheterized her. It took her two tries to talk. Her throat and mouth felt Sahara dry. "Money?" She was in one of those less than modest hospital gowns so figured someone had seen it and taken it. Hopefully someone honest.

"One of my brothers has it. He has a safe in his office; he put it in there for you. As soon as you're released, he'll bring it back to you." She nodded at him.

Morgan moved her hands to her lap and touched the needle on the back of her hand without letting him see what she was doing. She pulled it out gently and then, using the tape from the site, bent the tubing and taped it closed. Next, she moved her hand along the bed rail to find the controls to the bed.

Morgan's head was spinning, and making out the arrows and other icons on the thing made her a little lightheaded. She pushed one of the buttons and nearly screamed out loud when it stretched her out by lowering her flat. Quickly pushing another button had her rising up. She glanced over at him and noticed that while he was still sitting in the chair, he had now moved to a more alert position by sitting on the edge of the seat.

"You may not want to go too far up. You're pretty beat up. And with the broken ribs, it'll be painful."

It already was, she wanted to scream at him, but bit her lip to keep quiet. She had to stop once; fear of passing out from the shear intensity of pain had her taking in deep breaths until she could move again. When she was as far upright as she could physically stand, she stopped moving. It was another minute or two before she felt she could move on to the next phase of her plan.

Gingerly moving her feet to the side of the bed, she rolled and pushed herself into a sitting position in one movement. Stars danced behind her lids as she sat there, her back now to the man. He didn't say anything, but she heard his hiss of breath, then the deep chuckle. He had to see the other marks she was sure was there.

"There's a deep contusion on your left thigh that should keep you from standing, but at this point, I'd say it won't stop you from trying. It has a perfect print of a boot, so I'm guessing that someone kicked you there. The police took pictures. It's gonna hurt like hell when you get up. I say when because you are just stubborn enough to pull is off. So ... if you stand up without falling over, I'll kiss you. Damn, but you are one stubborn broad."

Morgan could hear the humor lacing his words. She wasn't out to prove anything to anyone. And if he came toward her with the intentions of kissing her, she'd make him regret that for many months to come.

Moving closer to the edge, she moved her right leg to the floor. It was tricky as the side rail to the bed was up and she seemed to be about seventy feet off the floor. When her toes touched the tile, she nearly cried with relief. Grasping the rail, she slowly moved her other leg down to be with its mate. She stood with all her weight on her right leg until she could get the pain under some sort of control and slowly, very slowly, began bearing weight on her left foot.

At first it didn't seem all that bad, and then, suddenly, pain shot from her toes to her hip like a knife stabbing the entire length. She bit her lower lip until she tasted blood. Dizzy now, she held onto the rail in a white-knuckle grip until she could breathe again. She opened her eyes and the man stood in front of her, concern written all over his face. She'd never heard him move.

"Let me help you back into bed, Ms. Becky, before the pain overwhelms you." When he reached out to touch her, she jerked back in terror. Her whimper had nothing to do with the pain this time, but the fear of the man. He must have realized it and took a hasty step back.

"Don't touch me. I...I don't know you. You need to back ... move away. Please." He took another step back and folded his arms over his massive chest. But he didn't stop watching at her.

Each step was an agonizing, mind numbing haze of pain. Putting most of her slight weight on the bed, she moved to the end, then across the foot to the top again. She had seen the little closet and was now making her way to it, praying that she'd make it without the support of the bed to hold her up. Concentrating on one step at a time, she leaned heavily on the door when she finally made it. Opening it up, and sobbing with untold happiness at finding her things there, she gathered them into her arm and, holding on to herself, moved to the bathroom.

Even though she knew it would feel wonderful, Morgan didn't sit on the commode. She didn't because she was terrified she'd not be able to get up again. Crying openly now that she was alone, she began the chore of getting first undressed then dressed again.

Taking off the gown, she nearly did sit. The bruises were horrific and many. She knew that some of them had happened today when Big Martha had attacked her, but some had happened when...well, she needed to get away from here before he came back and finished the job. She pulled her bloodied shirt from the pile of clothes and her bra. There was a little blood on it, but it was all she had. She put it on; luckily, the hook was in the front.

Morgan heard the man on the other side of the door talking. She couldn't hear what he was saying and, frankly, didn't really care. She'd be gone soon enough, and if they thought she was paying for this room, well, she couldn't afford it.

The loose-fitting pants—who was she kidding? Everything she owned fit her like it was too big—felt good and hardly rubbed the bruise at all. Her shoes were a problem, but she only slipped them on without even attempting to tie them. She could only brush her hair and let it hang long down her back. As soon as she could find some scissors, the shit was coming off. After brushing her teeth, she felt more human. She opened the door quietly and moved out into the room.

The doctor was sitting in the same chair as before. This time, however, he was positioned in front of the door. Well, fuck, so much for a clean get away.

"Move. You can't keep me here. I know my rights."

Morgan put as much hardness in her voice as she could, but all this moving and the pain had exhausted her. She was dizzier now than she had been, her leg was throbbing like a tooth ache, and she was pretty sure she was going to be sick.

"Actually, I can, as you see. I can't let you leave, Morgan. Not like this. You're eyes are glazed over with pain, you can barely walk without help, and you have nowhere to go. My mom will be here in a few seconds, as will my brothers. So pop a squat and we'll wait for the family to show up." He leaned his head back against the chair and grinned at her. Arrogant ass.

"This says I don't wait. Now move or one of us is going back to prison, and the other, the morgue." She watched as his eyes widened at the sight of the gun she was holding in her hand.

CHAPTER SEVEN

Damon stared at the gun, then at the woman. Damn, but she was feisty. He couldn't help it. He threw back his head and laughed. Still seemly lounging in the chair, he reached up and snatched the gun from her hand.

"If you're going to hold a gun on someone, you need to make sure that they can't see it's a squirt gun and it doesn't have an orange tip at the end. Now, get your happy ass in that bed before you fall over."

Damon watched her face. He looked for any sign that she was going to try something equally stupid as the gun, but she just stood there. When he stood up, she scrambled back several steps and he could see the pain this caused her, but he was either going to have to intimidate, or pick her up to get her into the bed. Neither was she going to like.

"I hate you." She stood there, glaring at him for a long time. He had to admit that she was pretty good at it, rivaled only by his mother. His mom could tear the skin right off of you with a look.

"Bed, Morgan, or I pick you up and put you there." The anger and fear that came into her eyes nearly made him relent, but he needed her to lie down before she fell down. She turned around and hobbled to the bed, her posture stiff and hard.

Morgan had just managed to get across the room when her

door flew open. His brothers never made anything but a grand entrance. His mom came in right behind them, fussing at Byron about his lack of pants without holes in them. She took one look at Morgan and turned her attention to her.

"Oh you poor baby. Come on now. Let's get you back to bed. Why is she dressed? You can't think you're going anywhere, not like this. Why, you can barely walk. Damon, what have you been doing to her?"

He just looked at his mom and scolded. "Me? I haven't done anything. I told her to stay in bed, and then she got up anyway. Which, I must say, impressed the hel…heck out of me. She is one stubborn little girl."

Damon grinned at Morgan when she looked ready to hit him. He simply couldn't help himself. Damn, but that girl had spunk.

"He didn't do anything but keep me here and I'm sure that wasn't his first idea. I want you people to leave me alone, damn it! I am a grown woman! You have to have another person you can annoy the shit out of because I have had enough. Now, get out! Fucking get out!"

Damon shifted his astonishment between the two women. His brothers were doing the same. He was sure at any moment the fireworks were going to start. And, damn, Nicky boy was missing it all.

"No, I don't have anyone right at the moment. You'll just have to put up with me. Boys, leave us, please. I'd like to talk to Morgan alone."

Damon looked over at Morgan and saw her turn her back on them. He wasn't sure if he should have been pissed or impressed with her. Once in the hall, he walked down to his brother's room to fill him in. Grinning like an idiot, he walked in Nicky's room and bellowed, "You are not going to fucking believe that girl!"

~~~

"Nicky, what the hell are you doing now?"

Damon had just relayed the fight between Ms. Becky and his mom and he expected him to just lie there? Not bloody likely.

"I'm going down there and kick her ass is what I'm gonna do. Move." Nick was out the door and down the hall before he had the last button done up on his robe. He was ten feet from the room when he heard the yelling. He nearly kicked in the door, but paused.

"I only want to help you! What is so hard to believe...?"

"Help me? Help me? I needed help five years ago, Mrs. Parker. Not now. I needed help when that bastard had me tied to the wall. When he raped me every fucking day for nine days. I needed help then when he sold me to his friends, giving them the opportunity to rape me as well. 'Have a little fun with the little cunt she has,' he said as a selling point. And when he tired of using his dick, he'd ram whatever was around into me, over and over until the blood would soak his hand. Do you know what this is? It's a perfect imprint of his teeth; yeah, he'd bite me hard enough to leave a reminder. I have several of them all over my body. Then there are the cigar burns, the lighter burns. He tried to set fire to my pubic hair once to see if it would burn faster than my head hair. Good thing the blood was too fresh to get it going, huh? Help me? I want to die, Ms. Parker. Will you help me with that?"

"That's enough." Nick didn't remember walking into her room, but was there suddenly. His mom looked like she had been pole axed, and Morgan looked defeated.

"Oh, Nickolas, I...I think..." He encircled his mom in his arms when she threw herself at him. He held her while she cried. He watched Morgan move to the bed and slowly work her way onto it. When she was able to get atop it, she pulled the sheet up to her chin and looked off into the room.

"Mom, go outside with Damon and the others. I'd like a few words with Morgan in private please." He pushed her along into his brother's arms and waited for them the close the door behind them before going over to the chair by the bed.

Nick didn't know what to say. No words, no thought, nothing. He sat there for several minutes before he thought he could speak.

"Do you need anything right now?" He winced at the question. How was she supposed to answer that? he wondered.

"Go away. I want to be left alone. Just, please go away." His heart clenched at the sound of her voice. It was broken and low, defeated and sad all at once.

"All right. For now. I'll be back as soon as I see to my mom. Morgan, I..." He watched as she rolled over to her other side and huddled under the blanket. She moaned softly, and he could tell that she was crying. Her shoulders were trembling.

For reasons he didn't want to think about, her tears bothered him more than his mother's had.

CHAPTER EIGHT

It was dark when Morgan woke up the next time. She hadn't meant to fall asleep, but she'd been crying and must have dozed off. Her whole body hurt, including her heart. She moved her leg gingerly and cried out at the pain shooting from the muscle in her thigh.

"Damon said you could have something for pain if you wanted it."

Nickolas Grant. What did she expect? He'd said he'd be back. His voice was coming from behind her, so she needed to turn over, but didn't really want to. She'd never been one to hide from something, but face it straight on. She moved slowly and stopped at her back; the pain was too much.

"I don't want anything. I can only go this far right now, and I don't know how long it will take me to get the rest of the way over, so if you wanna begin..."

"All right. There's a tray of food in front of you. Eat it while I talk." The light flared on and she shied away from it as best she could without moving too much. He was suddenly standing in front of her opening covers off of food.

Morgan wasn't going to eat anything, but didn't say anything. He'd just argue with her; she knew it, so she watched. When he had everything arranged, he slid the half table over in front of her, sat on the bed and picked up the fork. She turned her head from him.

"No. Say what you have to say then leave, Dr. Grant. I'm sure you have other things to do. I know I do." She heard him growl and nearly turned toward him, but didn't.

"You're not stupid. I've seen your transcript from college. So I won't even go into the reasons you need to keep your strength up by eating, how you'll heal much faster if your body isn't fighting starvation too." She heard the authority in his voice, the one that said, *you'll listen or else.* "This is the way this is going to work. I'm going to feed you this dinner and you're going to eat it or I call the nurse and we tie you down and put a tube down your throat and feed you that way. Up to you."

Morgan slowly turned back to him and glared. He was smiling with a sneer and still holding the fork. There was a small bite of something white on the end of it.

Opening her mouth, she took the bite. She decided she wasn't speaking to him. He could feed her, tell her off, because she was sure he was pissed at her treatment of his mother, and then he could leave.

"Damon will release you tomorrow morning. Byron will be here to pick you up and take you to an apartment that is in the Grant building that I own. He lived there up until a few months ago when he purchased his own home and had a studio built. The furniture is still there until the decorator he has doing his house decides what she wants to incorporate into the new house. I haven't the slightest clue what happens to the rest after he's finished.

"You'll also see a psychiatrist once a week starting next week. If she says you need more or less sessions, then you can work from there. If she says you need help and could benefit from others, then you'll get it. She will report to me every week on your progress and whether or not you show. She will not share what you talk about. I could care less anyway."

Morgan glared at him. What right did he have treating her like this? She wanted to scream at him. Just when she was opening her mouth to blast him, he jammed a forkful of food into her. Damned man.

"Monday morning, you'll start working for me as my receptionist/secretary. I'll pay you six fifty a week and you'll work Monday thru Friday and an occasional Saturday morning. Have no doubt that you'll work very hard for that, too. The rent for the apartment will be a part of your salary. As of Thursday, you have insurance, dental, medical, and vision. Here." He tossed a large envelope in her lap. "In that are your contract, medical information, and benefits. There's also a credit card with the company name on it. You'll use it for clothing and business needs. It's a generous amount, but not over the top, so use it wisely. Any questions?" Morgan watched him stand up and move the tray away. She had eaten everything on the plates. She wouldn't admit it to him, but she did feel a little better. But she wasn't going to work for him.

"No, and hell no. I'm not working for you, Dr. Grant. I don't need, nor do I want your charity, or whatever you feel this constitutes as. I'm quite capable of finding my…"

"Maybe you didn't hear the part about where I give a shit what you want because I don't, Ms. Becky. This is non-negotiable. According to the terms of your release, you find gainful employment within thirty days or they find it for you. For some reason, my mother likes you, and is concerned for your welfare. Well, I don't like you. You'll work for me starting Monday or else." He moved toward her door to leave. "One more thing, Ms.

Becky. If you *ever* talk to my mom that way again, I will hurt you."

Morgan pulled out the contract and read it over when her tray was taken away. It wasn't really anything special. She'd work for him for one year, with the option to renew after six months. Also included in her benefits was a week vacation after the six months. She may or may not have to do some light traveling, but it would be completely paid for by the Grant Corporation. There was also a copy of the paperwork she had signed when she'd been released from prison. In addition to her finding gainful employment, she needed to have a permanent residence. Apparently, he'd read it over as well.

For the first time in her life, she had a job making more money in one week than she had in her entire life. She had an apartment that was furnished with someone else's things in a building owned by the man she worked for and that hated her. A clothing allowance for things she didn't have a clue how to purchase much less how to use the credit card she'd been given to buy them, and she had never been more depressed in her life.

When Dr. Grant the physician came in at eight the next morning she was dressed and had her meager belongings packed. The contract was signed and in the required envelope to give to Byron when he came to get her. By two o'clock, she was standing alone in what she was now thinking of as another prison, one that just had nicer walls.

CHAPTER NINE

Morgan watched the women coming out of the building. She had gone to three different professional buildings since her hospital release two days ago to see if she could get an idea what she would be required to wear to work every day. Most of them wore pants and sweater sets with nice shoes. She looked down at her notes and saw that all the women she'd been observing were dressed the same. Now she needed to go and purchase the clothes.

Morgan had left the Grant building at around four, just after she'd taken an inventory of the rooms. It was just a place she was staying and she doubted it would ever be a home to her. She was now armed with her list of needs and her money. She had found it in another yellow envelope on the kitchen table when she had been shown around the apartment by Byron earlier that morning. She'd already decided to just get what she needed for now and would get the extras on other trips.

Morgan found a bus route map and, using it, made her way across town to the Wal-Mart. She got a cart and went to the clothing department and set about getting what she needed.

Only able to wear white panties and bras since she could remember, Morgan looked at the pretty colors the bras came in and it made her smile. Just who she would buy them for, she couldn't imagine, but bought a pink one with little lady bugs all over it for fun. Serviceable is what she needed, not fun, but she did it anyway.

The pants were a little tricky as she didn't have any idea what size she wore since she had been wearing the kind that tied at the waist. Taking several sizes in the changing room, she pulled them on and if they buttoned and zipped and weren't too long, they were her size, she figured. She had thought to only buy two pair, one black, the other blue, but the light gray ones were so nice that she got three. They were on clearance anyway so she didn't mind the extra cost. Next on her list were shirts. She found a nice silky T-shirt that came in lots of colors, so she picked out five of them, red, white, blue, green and lavender, and added them to her cart. She was able to find a white sweater and a nice plain black shirt on the clearance rack for only two dollars each and got them as well. Instead of getting pantyhose, which seemed like they'd be hot, she purchased a pair of black thigh highs and a sensible pair of black flat shoes. After getting herself a towel, a bag of apples, and a sleeping bag, she went up front to pay.

Two hundred and twenty-three dollars and twelve of those little plastic bags later, she was waiting at the bus stop. She was dizzy with exhaustion and hurt in places she'd only thought of. While she waited on the bus, she consolidated as much as she could. She put a lot of the clothing in her large bag. By the time the bus pulled up, she had managed to narrow it down to the sleeping bag she planned to use instead of the blankets and four very tightly packed little ones.

Morgan nearly missed her stop as she had dozed off for a minute and had only just gotten up to get off before the driver moved forward. Setting down her bags outside the Grant building door, she dug through her pockets to find her ID when

David opened the door for her and helped her in.

"Thank you very much, sir. I appreciate the help." She moved over to the elevators with her burdens and pushed the button to go up.

"Ms. Becky? I...I wanted to say how sorry I am about the other day. I shouldn't have grabbed at you. That just wasn't right. I just wanted to let you know, okay?" She looked up at the man and smiled. No one had ever told her they were sorry before.

"It's all right, Mr. Tulles. No harm done, really, at least not to me. I'm very sorry about your head. I didn't mean to hit you that hard." The doors opened for her and she hesitated just a moment before continuing. "I...I'm staying in Mr. Byron's apartment now. I work for Dr. Grant on the top floors. Just in case you see me around, I can be here now." Without waiting for him to reply, she stepped into the elevator and pushed the button for the fourth floor.

Later that night, after she'd taken a two hour nap, she sat looking out the window to the street below. She'd tried sleeping in the big bed, but she couldn't relax. She'd finally had to take her sleeping bag into the bathroom and put it in the tub. It was more what she was used to, the tightness of the room and there was only the door, no windows for anyone to get in. Now she was sitting at the kitchen table thinking about her life.

There was no family that she was aware of. She'd spent the first seventeen years of her life in a state run facility for homeless children. Morgan had never been adopted like most babies brought into the home. They had said it was her coloring. Her hair was a deep red and her eyes were the lightest blue, and her skin was so white it defied description. She was also tall for her age.

When Morgan looked in the mirror, she saw a woman,

not even a pretty woman at that. She'd heard people, women included, tell her she was beautiful, but she just didn't see it.

Morgan worked hard and stayed to herself even as a small child. She discovered early she had a photographic memory and could learn languages very quickly. That had served her well throughout high school and her little bit of college she'd taken on the outside. Then when she was able to, she had taken classes to finish up her degree and now had a BA in business management. Not that it had done her a lot of good. Once people saw that she had been an inmate of the State Pen, they stopped right there.

Morgan reflected on her life on the inside. She'd spent the first eighteen months in the infirmary. Having been raped and beaten as badly as she had, it was months before she could even walk very far. Then there was the two self-inflicted gunshot wounds, one to her head the other to her left shoulder. Her hand had taken the longest to heal. She had broken it in four different places that night so that she could get the cuff off her wrist to escape.

Randall Bennett had told her that she was going to die. She hadn't cared at that point whether or not she did, but he was definitely going to. When he had left her to go upstairs to get his gun, she had begun slamming her hand hard against the wall between the cot headboard and the wall.

After the first two breaks, she pretty much hadn't felt the other two and with the help of her blood, was able to get her right hand out of the cuff and drop to the floor, sliding the whole cuff out of its hanger. Dizzy from pain and exhaustion, she crawled to the door and waited for him.

When he came through the door, she tripped him and took his gun. It took her two tries to get the gun's trigger to work; then she simply pulled it seven times and killed him. When the police arrived after a neighbor had called in the sound of gunshot, she was just putting the gun under her chin for the third time. The first shot had gone awry and a ricochet had caught her in the shoulder. The second time, she'd let the gun slip and it grazed her head in a deep cut. The young officer begged her to stop and, in the end, had had to shoot her himself to prevent her from killing herself.

There hadn't been a day that went by that she wished either his aim had been worse, or hers better.

CHAPTER TEN

Nick didn't expect her to show. It mattered little that she had signed the contract and had taken the apartment; he knew her type. He looked down at the file his investigator had given him yesterday at home and frowned. Well, he amended, he thought he knew her type.

The detective had managed to dig up her entire file, including pictures of her arrest and her penal file. He couldn't for the life of him understand why she had been convicted in the first place. She had obviously been a victim of the first order. She hadn't even been able to attend her own trial as she had been so severely injured that she had been put into a medical coma for nearly three months to heal. He was sure if she'd have had Devin as her lawyer, she never would have seen the inside of a cell.

Nick had told her to be here at eight o'clock and he had come in at six-thirty wanting to get caught up as much as he could. He heard her in the outer office talking to David at six-fifty. He went to his office door and leaned against the jamb, listening to them.

"If that door gives you anymore issues, just call downstairs and I'll have facilities see to it for you. No telling how long you'd have been stranded in there if'n I hadn't been doing my walk then."

"Thanks, Mr. Tulles. I was really grateful to see you. Thank you again." David saw him first, and she jerked around when he straightened up and looked over her shoulder.

"Morning, Dr. Grant. Ms. Becky had herself some problems with the door on the stairwell." David tipped his hat at the man and left.

Nick watched her walk to the little break area that the previous secretary had insisted on having, and listened to the cabinet open then close. He assumed she was putting her lunch away and she'd be out soon. He waited for five more minutes before he went to see what she was doing and nearly plowed her over when she finally came out.

"I'm sorry. I was...good morning, Dr. Grant. I'll just get started." She moved around him and toward the desk. She was carrying that huge ass bag with her, but other than that, she looked...very nice. He also noticed that she was still limping. Not as badly as in the hospital, but noticeably.

"Do you need more time off? Let me take you down to see Damon. He's a good doctor and this could be serious. I won't have you falling over here and claiming Workman's Comp." He saw her stiffen at his words.

"Thank you for your nice concern, Dr. Grant, but I'll be just fine."

He flushed; he'd been neither nice nor concerned-sounding. He hadn't meant for it to come out quite like that and felt bad. "Ms. Becky, Morgan, I didn't..." He didn't know what he'd been about to say, but she cut him off.

"Mrs. Wayne will be here soon. She's going to set me up on the computer with email and things. She asked me to have you make a list of the things you'd like me to have access to of yours. I believe she mentioned your appointment calendar and scheduler."

Nick knew he was being dismissed, but didn't know how to get out of it. He'd been an ass and she wasn't going to say anything. *Fine!* If that's the way she wanted it, then he'd go back in his office.

Nick sat at his desk for a solid three hours not doing a damned thing. He did look online and booked Morgan a day at the spa. He didn't tell her, of course, but he did mark it on the calendar that they would share. He felt stupid for his earlier comments and wanted to make up for it. When there was a knock at his door, he bellowed for whoever it was to enter. He was surprised to see his brother Byron.

"I can see you haven't had your morning Joe yet. Wanna go down to the corner and get some? My treat." He had flopped down in one of the wingback chairs that faced his desk and put his feet up.

"No. I have to make a list of things that my new secretary might need of mine. You know, calendars and appointments for scheduling for me. Rachel is going to set her up with her system today." Why he sounded so petulant, he didn't know.

"Rachel Wayne? She just left. Maybe Morgan didn't need your list after all. Come on, go down with me. I need to have an old man with me so I look better to the new waitress they got. She has nice...yeah. Go with me." Nick stood to leave and go with him when his cell phone went off.

"Hello! Grant." Christ! He needed to get a grip. First mean, then grouchy, now he was barking.

"Hello to you too. I was wondering if Morgan came in today. I...I wanted to make sure she was settling in all right with you." His mom. She had been upset since he'd told her that he'd hired her and the conditions he'd put on her, including her not speaking to her like that again.

"I guess. Rachel came over and just set her up. Whether she stays or not is anyone's guess. Byron and I are going down to the corner for some coffee and women. Want me to bring you by anything?"

"Yes, thank you. I'd like a busty blonde, hold the large hips. And bring me one of those caramel nutty buns too."

Nick smiled. He wondered if any other mother in the world was anything like her, and doubted it. She was definitely one of a kind.

"I'll see what I can do." He was walking toward the door as he hung up. When he opened it, Morgan wasn't at her desk. He knew instinctively that she hadn't left; her pink bag was still laying there where she had put it when she came in. They were getting on the elevator and headed down when he realized he hadn't asked her if she wanted anything. Oh well, he'd get her a nutty bun too.

He and Byron spent an enjoyable hour in the coffee shop. After his second cup of plain coffee, he felt measurably better. He had them box up three of their buns, two for his mother in one box, and one for Morgan in another. He then set off to see his mom. On the drive over, he'd had his artistic brother draw her her busty woman with tiny hips on her box.

"I don't suppose you forgot to give Morgan your cell phone number before we left, did you?" Byron said. Well, fuck! No wonder she'd not called him. She couldn't reach him.

CHAPTER ELEVEN

"Grant Corporations, Morgan Becky speaking. May I help you?" Her voice sounded okay, Morgan thought. She hadn't known what to say when the phone had rang earlier this morning, but Ms. Wayne had scribbled down the words quickly for her. It was nearly two-thirty now and she'd spent a pleasant morning getting set up and learning her job.

It was fairly easy so far. Dr. Grant had called at eleven, gave her his cell phone number, and made sure she repeated it to him four times before he'd hung up. He'd called twice more since then. She'd taken seven phone messages and made him two appointments for the following day.

Morgan had found the spa day that he'd set up for her then She kept going back to it and couldn't for the life of her think what it had meant. He'd put her name, correct this time, and "day at spa" with the name of the place. It would probably be really nice, but she didn't want to make a fool of herself and scream when someone touched her. Morgan decided that he was really sweet to do it. Strange, but sweet.

Ms. Wayne had given her the direct number to her desk, and if she needed anything, to just call. Ms. Wayne had also left her a large book of information on the company. It told her what Dr. Grant was a doctor of, finance, and how much money he was presumably worth, seventy million and counting. It had also told of his wife's tragic death fourteen months into their marriage in a car accident that had also taken the life of his father.

"Nicky there? I need to talk to him. Tell him it's Bambi." The voice on the other end sounded just like a person would think a Bambi'd sound like. All high-pitched and squeaky voiced.

"I'm sorry, Ms. Bambi, but Dr. Grant isn't in right now. But if you'd like, I can take a message and give it to him when he returns." There wasn't a sound for so long. She could hear her breathing, a mouth breather, so she knew she hadn't hung up.

"Did he tell you not to ring me through? I don't like to be put off and he damned well knows it. Put him on the phone or tell him I'm a'coming down there to see him." Suddenly, Bambi sounded less like a Bambi, and more like a barracuda.

"No. He's not here. But like I said, if I can take a message for you, I'll make sure he..." Morgan hadn't just been cut off, but snapped off like a twig.

"I'll be down there in ten minutes. You tell him so." And the phone was suddenly whining at her.

The first thing she did was call David at the front desk. She warned him that a Ms. Bambi was coming in with a full head of steam and demanding to speak to Dr. Nickolas Grant. Then, as much as she hated to, she called the man himself.

"Dr. Grant, its Morgan Becky. A Ms. Bambi is on her way to the office looking for you. She wanted to speak to you. I've made her aware that you aren't in, but that didn't seem to stop her. I have let David know of her impending arrival and her... hummm, mood, as well. Thank you." Then, she hung up. She didn't want to tie up his line, nor the company line, and stated what she needed to.

Looking at the caller ID, Morgan was surprised that Dr. Grant was calling back. "Grant Corporations, Morgan Becky speaking. May I help..." She was surprised when he was nearly spitting he was so angry.

"Don't you ever fucking hang up on me ag..." She put the phone back on its cradle. When it rang again, she almost didn't answer it, but gave in. Maybe it wasn't him.

"Grant Corporations, Morgan..."

"I swear to Christ, if you fucking hang up..." She hadn't done anything wrong and didn't believe he had the right to talk to her like that. It wasn't the language. She'd been in prison and heard much worse. It was his tone. She hung up again. After the fourth time, he let her answer before he said anything.

"Grant Corporations, Morgan Becky speaking. May I help you?" She knew it wasn't him as soon as she put the receiver to her ear.

"Morgan, I would suggest you not hang up on him again. His face is a shade of purple I've never seen before. Plus, you should see the foam coming from the corner of his lips." Byron's voice was heavily laced with ill suppressed humor.

"Then tell him to talk to me in a civil tone, or not to call at all. I gave him the information he needed. I'm not very good at cell phones and such. They weren't very prevalent when I went in the joint and I'm trying to get used to them. I've had a really good day up until now and he's not going to come back here and ruin it. So tell him I said to fuck off, it's six-thirty and I'm going home." She hung up the phone again and shut down his computer. Turned off the lights, locked the door and walked down the ten flights of stairs to Byron's apartment. When she got to the correct floor, she couldn't get out. The flipping door jammed again. She sat down on the stairs and started crying.

CHAPTER TWELVE

The next morning, Nick noticed that she was walking with more of a pronounced limp. He started to ask her about it, but one look at her face told him he'd live longer if he didn't. Since she'd come in at seven-thirty, she'd not spoken a single word to him and it was nearly five-thirty now. The only time he'd heard from her was in email form and that was to give him an update to his schedule change she'd made in regards to a cancelled appointment. Oh, and there was the mumbled thank you when he'd given her her check at lunch time.

He realized he was hiding in his office at six, waiting for her to leave, when he heard the door close to the main area. Nick had never hidden from a woman in his life, especially one who worked for him.

He was just slipping on his jacket when his cell phone rang. Overseas call, he thought, and answered with his first smile of the day.

"Bonjour, my friend. How's France treating you?" He really liked André Marcus, and was genuinely glad to hear from him.

"Ha, Nickolas! I was hoping to get your little cupcake. She is gone for the day, yes? I sometimes forget the time changes." *Cupcake*?

"Yes, but Marie no longer works for me, I'm sorry to say. I

have a new person." He would have thought André would have called before now and known about Morgan.

"Yes, yes. Morgan. Ah, she must be a vision. She speaks French like it is her native tongue. I have so enjoyed speaking with her. She is very knowledgeable, that one. I hope you keep her. Why, I have spent more money on the market since she has been helping me with the paintings than I did before just to hear her lovely voice. You must send me a photo of her, so that I may dream the dreams of little boys about her."

Nick sat down hard in his chair. She spoke French? And helped with thirteenth century paintings? And he wasn't even going to think about what he meant about dreaming about her.

"You've talked to Morgan? In French?" He heard André chuckle and felt himself blush. She worked for him and he knew nothing about her. It was all her fault, too, going all day without saying a word. Of course, he'd been hiding in his office all day and, which would not allow conversation. He was becoming an idiot over a woman.

"Oui. I'm thinking I shall need to come to the United States and see this girl for myself if she has the great Nickolas so flustered he doesn't listen to her voice. Maybe I will come and steal her away back to Paris with me. She will make a nice addition to my collection, no?"

"No, I mean, no, you can't have her. I...did you need anything from me, André?" The two men talked for a little while longer and made a time for next week to meet for dinner when Nick was going to be in Paris for an estate sale.

He was still stewing about it when he got downstairs to the main lobby and David stepped in front of him. He'd apparently been trying to get his attention for some minutes.

"I'm sorry, David. My mind is all over the place. What can I do for you? Wait, I thought you got off at four on Fridays." For some reason, it bothered him that he knew that. He knew the man in the lobby's schedule, but nothing about the woman who worked beside him every day for the past few days.

"Yes, sir. I wanted to come in and tell you how sorry I am about Ms. Becky. I should have called the workmen right away, but I thought it was a fluke. I should have known better. Her having to spend all night in that stair well, I got them out here right away this morning, sir. She won't have any more issues with that anymore." He didn't think he could handle any more problems with Morgan "Cupcake" Becky tonight, but asked anyway.

"I'm sorry, I had to go to the police station last night and file a complaint about Bambi Jenkins. I must have missed what happened with her. What did she do now?" He was rubbing his chest again. The burning was nearly up to his throat and he wanted a drink of water in the worst way.

"The door jammed again. She came down the stairs after work last night and couldn't get out of the well. Jeffrey didn't find her until after midnight when he was walking the stairs. Poor thing couldn't hardly walk, her all kinked up and all. But he didn't touch her, no sir. I told them all not to. Must have been in there for about six hours, I figured. But the door's fixed up. I wanted you to know that personally." Nick could only stare at him for a few seconds. Then he thanked him for taking care of the situation.

Morgan had hung up on Byron at six-thirty and Jeffrey hadn't found her until after midnight. Six hours. He suddenly realized why she was limping more pronounced today. She'd probably been sitting on the stairs waiting for someone to come and get her. And why wasn't she using the elevator, for Christ's sake?

It was right there. Or her cell phone? Come to think of it, did he even have her cell phone number? No, he did not, he realized. Stubborn woman.

Well, she had a phone; he'd had it installed before she'd moved in. He started dialing her phone number in her apartment as he made his way to his car. It just rang and rang. Okay, it was Friday night; maybe she went to get her something to eat, a pizza or something. It was payday, she probably had things to do, he decided. Maybe she had a date. No, not a date. She wouldn't be on a date. *She'd better not be on a date*, he thought furiously. Frowning, he considered why she couldn't be on a date and that he didn't want her to and decided she just couldn't be. She was getting a pizza to bring home.

~~~

"I'm sorry, Ms. Morgan, but your credit history is non-existent. You can't open a checking account, or any other account, without a credit report." This was the third bank she'd been to tonight. Her first paycheck and it might as well have been a tissue for all the good it was doing her.

"You do realize that I can't have a credit history without first having credit, don't you? I mean, no one will give me a credit card without a checking account. Without a credit card, I can't open a checking account. Do you see where this is going?"

Morgan's head hurt. And the woman was looking at her as if she didn't have a clue what she was talking about. Or, more likely, that she didn't care. She had her rules and she was following them, damn it.

Morgan left the bank and went to the bus station. She only had seventy-five dollars left of the money she'd gotten from the prison and if she couldn't cash her check, she'd not be able to eat. She'd never used the company credit card because the first time she had pulled it out, she realized she didn't have a clue how much the limit was, if it had a pin, or if they had to call Dr. Grant to get it approved. So she put in back in her wallet and paid cash. The card was now in the freezer in Byron's apartment.

Morgan stared out at the building across from her and it took her a few minutes to realize what the sign said. She walked across the street and went into the bar. There was a seedy-looking man at the bar and two half-naked women dancing on the stage.

"Hi. I was wondering about the bartending job that you have advertised. I was hoping I could fill out an application." The bartender looked at her, up then down. After focusing on her breasts and licking his lips, he looked at her face.

"Might make more money on the stage if'n those are real." He looked down again as if judging if he could get away with testing the realness of them.

"No, thanks. Just the bar please. I used to tend a while ago, hummm about five years now, I guess." She wanted to leave, take a hot bath, and then burn her clothes. But she needed money she could get to now.

"Okay, you're hired. You fuck up, and you'll be out the door right quick. Mr. Mick don't cotton to no slackers. Can you start right now? We'll be getting the Friday night crowd in soon and I need someone tonight."

Tucking her bag behind the bar and putting on an apron, Morgan began her career as a tap maid

~~~

Her first doctor's appointment was the next morning. Dr. Mercer had been all right with scheduling it for then. She said that she knew what it was like to work full time and try to have a life too.

"How are you sleeping at night? I've read your file. I know

that you had frequent nightmares while you were inside." She was a pretty lady, Morgan thought. Her office was done up in summery colors of reds and blues. There wasn't a couch to lie down on, which she was profoundly glad for. She sat in a regular chair across the desk from her as they got to know each other.

"All right. Nothing much to report." She'd actually had a nightmare every night since moving into Byron's apartment, but she wasn't telling anyone any more than she had to. She'd had a shrink in prison, and had learned the hard way not to say things you didn't want everyone on the block to know.

"You don't trust me. That's okay, you have no reason to. But I am here to help you adjust. Nick said that you were coming here under conditions of your release. That isn't completely true. You are free. You've been completely exonerated of all the charges against you. You won't be going back." Morgan just looked at her. She knew that when he'd told her, but she also needed a job.

They sat there for several minutes before Dr. Mercer spoke again. Morgan could, and had, gone for days without speaking to another human; the quiet didn't bother her.

"Would you tell me about the rape, Morgan? I know that something like that can have a profound effect on someone, and sometimes talking about it can make it seem less intense."

"No." She waited for the threats or the soothing tones to get her to talk. She wasn't going to have share time with a perfect stranger.

"Then can you tell me about working for Dr. Grant? He is a very good-looking man, and I've heard his brothers are equally good-looking. Tell me about him."

"No. If you want a date with him, call me on Monday and I'll make you an appointment. I want to go. I've been here long enough." She stood now and walked to the door. She fully expected to be stopped, but Dr. Mercer didn't say anything other than she'd see her next Saturday at the same time.

CHAPTER THIRTEEN

Nick tried calling her ever thirty minutes all weekend. By Monday morning, he was not a happy man. It was small wonder that when she walked in the office that morning, he lit into her like a mad man.

"Where the fuck have you been? I've been trying to contact you all weekend and you didn't answer your phone." He was so furious that he didn't even wait until she put down that ridiculous pink bag. It occurred to him over the weekend that he was jealous and he didn't understand or like it. Not one bit.

"I don't have a phone." She turned her back on him, put her bag down, and went into the little break area. He stood there for all of thirty seconds and stormed after her.

"Yes, you do. Now, I want to know where you were that you were too busy to answer it." He could hear himself and realized how stupid he was sounding. He wanted to shake her, and make her pay attention to him.

"I'm really tired, Dr. Grant, and I think I'd remember if I heard a phone ring. You have three appointments this morning and another two this afternoon there..."

"I don't give a flying fuck about the appointments. Come with me." When he reached for her arm, she jerked back so suddenly she fell into her desk and nearly knocked over the computer.

"Don't touch me. I've told you before; I don't like to be touched. I have work to do. What do you want?" For the first time, he noticed the dark circles under her eyes and the bruise on her jaw.

"What's wrong with you? What happened to your face? Did someone hit you?" He found himself wanting to protect her and spank her at the same time.

"Yes. Now, what is it you want? I don't have a phone. I don't want a phone. And I don't know what you're talking about." She turned on the computer to begin her day.

"Come with me. I'm going to show you the phones. And you didn't properly answer my questions. Who hit you?" They were making their way to the private elevators as he spoke. When he pushed the button, he noticed she was gone and the stairwell door was closing. What the hell...?

He started to follow her and just then the doors opened. He stepped inside and decided to wait for her down there. Just as he stepped off the lift, his brother Byron was standing there.

"Hey, I was just coming to see you. Where you going?" He was still moving his things out of the studio and into his own. Nick could see the last of the crates being loaded onto the service elevator.

"That stupid woman says there is no phone in her apartment. I've come down to prove it to her. She didn't pick up all weekend. What if I needed her to go and get something out of the office for some reason? How would she have known to go and get it?" The object of his disdain was just coming through the door as he finished.

"Hello, Mr. Grant. Thank you for the use of your apartment. I don't believe I've had the opportunity to thank you before." She moved to the door and unlocked it. Then she stood back for both men to enter ahead of her.

Nick pulled out his cell phone and hit redial. He looked at her with a sneer as he waited for the ringing to begin.

"Morgan, would you mind if I had a look around to see what else is here that I can use at the house? I promise not to disturb anything." *Flirt,* Nick thought. *Always flirting.*

"It's your apartment, Mr. Grant. Look at anything you want. I'm waiting for the phones to start ringing. I don't know what he's about. I've never heard a phone in here since I started staying here." She moved to the kitchen and sat down at the table to wait.

Nick could hear the phone ringing in his ear, but nothing in the little apartment. He went to the bedrooms and then all through the living room, having to call a second, then a third time when it cut him off saying there was no answer and to call again.

"I know I had phone service installed the day before you moved in here. Where are the phones?" He looked at her; he was tapping his foot as he waited.

"I don't have any phones because I don't have any service. If you had them install service, they didn't leave any phones here. Thus, I don't have phone service. How am I suppose to know there is a ringing phone if there isn't a phone to hear, you moronic jackass? If you plan to half-ass a job, then you should expect half-assed results. I have work to do. Lock up when you leave, or don't. I could care less." She nearly bowled over Byron as he entered the kitchen and with a mumbled apology, she slammed out of the apartment.

"You handled that with grace and aplomb. Congratulations, big brother, you've officially become a class A ass." He watched as Byron left the apartment too.

They were right; he was becoming unhinged. He flopped

down in the kitchen chair she had just left and rubbed his chest. He couldn't for the life of him figure out what was wrong with him. He pulled out his cell and called Damon.

"I think I need to see you. I can't...my chest is burning and I can't eat again." Ten minutes later, he was walking into his brother's office to get checked out.

CHAPTER FOURTEEN

Morgan was on the phone when he came back upstairs two hours later. She didn't even glance at him when he laid the bag from the local phone store on the desk and a small container with an African violet in it. Nick didn't think that she'd like roses. He didn't know why. Besides, he thought the planter would look pretty on her desk. He stood there waiting for her, then finally moved to one of the chairs as she finished up the call.

"I'm sorry. There are four phones in there. You can put them wherever you'd like." She raised an eyebrow at him and he amended his statement. "Anywhere in your apartment you'd like. I'm sorry I didn't tell you about the service being hooked up."

"Wow! That must have hurt. The great Dr. Nickolas Grant says he's sorry. The world will surely come to a halt." She didn't care what he thought at this point.

"There's no need to be snarky. I just assumed that you'd figure out if there weren't any phones in the place, you might need to get some. How the hell was I supposed to know you were that dense?"

"Well, that certainly didn't last long, did it? I have the phones Dr. Grant; I'll plug them in as soon as I get downstairs. Is there anything else I can fuck up for you today? No? Then I'll get back to work." She picked up the phone on the third ring and dismissed him with a turn of the chair.

"Good morning, Grant Corporations, Morgan Becky speaking. May I help you?"

"Hello, Morgan. It's Margaret Parker. I was wondering if you'd meet me for dinner tonight? I can meet you anywhere you'd like." Just friggin' great. If this day could get any worse, she didn't have a clue how. She looked up at Nick and sighed. *Yeah,* she thought, *I guess it could.*

"Ms. Parker, I…" She saw him tense up when she mentioned his mother's name. He was waiting for her to say something mean. Little did he know, she didn't have any meanness left in her today. He'd taken care of that all on his own.

"Please, Morgan. I've got some things to say to you, some things I should have said before. Please?"

"All right, Ms. Parker, I'll meet you. I should get out of here around six, barring any unforeseen problems." *Like I have to murder your son.*

"Good, I'll meet you out front of the Grant building at six-thirty. Thank you, dear, I'll see you then."

She hung up the phone and dared the man across from her to say a word. Any would set her off, and she knew it. Apparently, so did he, because he got up and went to his office without uttering a single one. Damned man.

Morgan was standing outside the building when the large limo pulled up. When the driver came around to the sidewalk side and opened the door, Morgan looked around for the rider. When Ms. Parker called to her from the depths of it, she walked forward.

"Come in, dear. I so hate to drive and this was free for the day." The driver handed her inside and she sat across from her boss's mother.

"Ms. Parker. I don't know what you could say to me here that you couldn't say over the phone. You didn't need to have dinner with me." She was uncomfortable, first, because she was in a limo, and secondly, because of who she was with.

Morgan kept expecting Nick to come out to the desk and to tell her to be nice, or some other such advice, all afternoon. But he'd stayed in his office and didn't even come out when she'd left for the day. She didn't really care what he did in there; she was just glad he'd chosen to leave her alone.

"I wanted to tell you how sorry I am. I was out of place the other week and I've felt bad about it since. Nicky told me what he'd said to you afterwards and I've told him what I think of him interfering, as well. I want us to be friends, Morgan. I really do."

She didn't want any friends. Friends wanted things she no longer could give people. Trust and understanding were just a few of the things.

"I don't... I'm not sure how to be a friend, Ms. Parker. I like just being alone and on my own. I'm not...you're out of my league, and I...I just want to be left alone."

"Out of my league? What nonsense. I'm just a normal person, just as you are. Why would you think I'm out of your league?"

"Well, for one thing, money. Secondly, and I think this is the big one; you've never spent time in prison. That in of itself is usually what separates the humans from sub humans."

"Morgan, do you think of yourself as a sub human? Oh, child, what happened to you wasn't your fault. You were a victim. You weren't to..."

"Ms. Parker. I'm here because you asked me to be. I killed that man as surely as you're sitting here. Does it make it okay because of what he did? Am I justified in taking his life? No. At least, I don't think so. Yes, he deserved to be punished, but death, that wasn't my call to make. I wish some days, most days really, that I was still back in prison. I understood it there. There were rules, sects, and people left me alone. In the five years, six months, two weeks, and four days I was in there, I had one visitor, you. In the two months I've been out...I wish I could go back."

Morgan turned to the window and watched the buildings go by. She wasn't hoping for sympathy, nor was she asking for forgiveness. She truly wanted to be left alone.

"I'm very sorry you feel that way, child. I really am. I wish I could make it better for you, tolerable anyway."

She heard the sadness in her voice and turned back to the older woman. "It wasn't my intention to make you sad, Ms. Parker. Let's have a nice dinner, all right? I've never been out before. Where are we going?"

After a few minutes of tense silence, Ms. Parker looked at her. "Chinese. I love it. Have you ever eaten it? I'm not sure anything they would have served you in the big house would be considered food, much less an ethnic group."

"Big house?" Morgan laughed, hard and long. "Okay, the big house only served three types of meals—firm, mushy, and deep fried. Oh, and then there was dessert. Mostly it was fruit, but sometimes, we'd have green pie, black pie, or my favorite, yellow sponge. Some days I'd take mine back to the cell and use it for bathing."

"Morgan Becky! Did you just make a joke?" The two women laughed uproariously the rest of the way to the restaurant and through most of their dinner.

CHAPTER FIFTEEN

"Tomorrow is Thanksgiving; are you brining anyone to Mom and Dan's? Mom invited Morgan, but she isn't coming. Mom is fairly disappointed about it." Byron had come into town to have dinner with Nick and to start trying to get ideas for Christmas presents.

"No, I don't normally think of Thanksgiving as a 'bring a date' kind of holiday. Why, did you have someone in mind?"

Nick hadn't been on a date in months. Not even to get laid. Damon had him on this low fat, low cholesterol, no taste diet and it was killing his energy level. Plus, he...fighting with Morgan was wearing him out too.

"Nah, just wondering. I was dating this woman from *Charlie's*, but that didn't pan out. She wasn't into the same relationship needs I was, so we called it quits." Nick stared at his brother. He didn't think he'd ever heard the term "relationship needs" uttered out of his mouth before.

"You mean she wanted long term and you wanted sex. Yes, I can see where that would be an issue for you. Come on, we're supposed to meet Damon at his office at six and I'm starving."

Both men got up to leave, but Nick hesitated for just a few minutes more. He didn't want to get into it with Morgan again. He just couldn't seem stop picking at her. He knew that's what he was doing, but it didn't stop him from doing it.

"She's gone."

Nick looked sharply at his brother. He felt his face heat up. Damn it, how'd he figure it out?

"I...what are you talking...what do you mean she's gone? It's not even six yet. She's supposed to stay until...well, I don't even know when she normally leaves, but it's never before me." He was unreasonably pissed now. Damn it, he was leaving. Why shouldn't she be able to?

"She was leaving when I came in an hour ago. Said she had some things she had to do before she had to go out again. Don't know, didn't ask, and didn't care. Why do you? I mean, it's not like she doesn't work like sixty hours a week anyway. Back off, give her some air. You know, Nicky, if you hate the girl so much, why don't you just get rid of her?" Nick was glad that Byron was in front of him, because the thought of getting rid of Morgan startled him for a few seconds.

"Because we have a contract, and besides, she does a good job. At least she hasn't fucked up that I know of. Good secretaries are very hard to find." They were going down in the elevator to the first floor as they talked. Besides, he thought, his mom would probably shoot him if he did. For some reason, the two of them got along great.

The doctor's office was beginning to be decorated for Christmas as it was closed from now until the Monday after Thanksgiving. The staff was also having a little celebration as they worked. Nick wondered if he should have Morgan put up a tree and then dismissed the idea. No one came to their offices and he didn't know what her plans were anyway.

"Hello, Nicky, long time no see. I've been thinking a lot about you lately." Marsha Bentley always made him feel like he was a slab of meat on a hook. She looked at him like that too.

She was pretty enough, he supposed, with her bottle dark hair and full lips, but she wasn't...he didn't want to think about what she wasn't. But she wasn't, not at all. He'd been thinking about redheads a lot lately. Not that Morgan had anything to do with it. He'd always liked red heads, with their creamy skin, and her freckles across...their freckles, not hers. Freckles across the nose were a natural on redheads, not just on Morgan. Damned woman, it was all her fault he couldn't get laid.

"I'm fine." He realized he'd barked at her when she looked at him with raised eyebrows. Byron was giving him the same look. He turned to find Damon. People were reading too much into everything he'd done lately.

"Damon, you about ready to go?" He started to rub his chest again and stopped short. He'd been told if he didn't have any more flare ups, he could have a regular dinner tomorrow. He was not ruining that now.

"Dr. Grant there's a woman on the...oh, hello, Dr. Grant. Happy Thanksgiving! Hummm...there's a woman on the phone, says she has a piece of glass in her foot and can't get it out. Want me to transfer it in here?" Tansy Bell was the oldest woman working for Damon, and the most dedicated too.

"A piece of glass? Tell her how to get it out and then to glue it shut if it's bigger than half an inch long," Damon told Tansy without bothering to look up from what he was doing.

Nick sat across from his brother's desk when Tansy shut the office door. Damon was still filling out charts and said he'd only be a few more minutes.

"Glue it shut? That's a new one. Just use regular old Elmer's?" Nicky leaned up and took a cigar out of the box on his desk as he spoke. He didn't light it up, really didn't like to smoke them, but the smell ... ahhhh, that was ambrosia to him.

"No, super glue. It works pretty well on smaller cuts. It cleans the wound, too, with the eucalyptus in it. They've been using it at the hospital for years. Get your feet off my desk, you heathen." They both turned to the door when Tansy popped back in.

"I'm sorry, sir, but it's Ms. Becky. She said that she doesn't have any tweezers and she doesn't think that will work anyway. She has the glue, but she just can't get it out. Want me to go up and help her? She's such a nice little thing." She already had her coat on and they could hear the others leaving as well. Nick looked at Damon and sighed.

"I'll go up and take care of her. You go on home, Tansy, and you" — he pointed at Damon — "had better be ready when I get back."

Nick took the stairs two at a time and was looking forward to blasting the perfect Ms. Becky. How she could not get a sliver of glass out of her foot was beyond him. He stopped suddenly, unless she was trying to make her move toward Damon. Nah, Damon wasn't her type. She'd be more...well, his type if he was looking for a woman, which he wasn't.

By the time he got to her door, he had worked himself up into quite a snit. He had her moving in with Damon and having Devin's love child and raising Meggie, Spencer's little girl, all at the same time. When he found the door partly open, he threw it back against the wall with enough force to knock a picture off the opposite wall. He knew the moment the sound reverberated in the room that he shouldn't have done it. Everything about her screamed for him to protect her, but all he could seem to do was push her away.

"Morgan Becky, where the hell are you, and why is your door open for just any one to walk in?" When she came through the door from the kitchen, he nearly swallowed his tongue. Christ, where the hell did she think she was going dressed like that?

"Where's your brother, the doctor? The real doctor. I want him to come up and fix this." He stalked toward her and noticed that she'd been crying.

"He's busy, and he's not your type anyway. Let me see this piece of glass so that he and I can get going."

"No. I want you to leave. I...you won't be nice, and I hurt too much to hold my mouth closed. Please, you leave. I'll...I don't know what I'll do, but I want you to leave." He noticed she was leaning against the doorjamb and her foot was up behind her.

"Damon is busy. I'm going to take the glass out, glue it closed, and you're going to tell me where you think you're going dressed like a street walker on a Wednesday night."

She turned around and hopped back into the kitchen, of course not answering him. She did that a lot; he thought — didn't answer when he asked her something. Well, damn it, she wasn't walking away now.

Nick walked into the room and nearly hit the floor. He looked down and was startled by the amount of blood on it. He looked up at Morgan, who was trying to climb up onto the sink, when he noticed that the blood was pouring from her foot, her shoed foot. And sticking right out of the top and bottom was a hunk of glass glossy with her blood. His heart went into overdrive seeing her hurt. The need to cradle her in his arms and to keep her safe, paramount.

"Mother fuck! What did you do?" He picked her up at once and settled her on the counter with her foot in the sink. He ignored her protests about being touched and gently lifted her foot up to get a closer look.

The glass was approximately three inches long, about an inch wide, and about four inches high. He looked at her and nearly crumbled with shame. She had been crying, and she still was.

"It hurts. Can you take it out? I have the glue Ms. Tansy said to glue it with. If you could get it out, I can do the rest so you can go to your mom's." Nick hated himself more in that moment than he had ever hated himself before. He pulled out his cell phone and called Damon.

"I need you up here *right now*! And bring your bag of tricks. She's hurt badly and I think she might have lost a great deal too much blood."

CHAPTER SIXTEEN

"Come on, darling, lean back. I need to numb this area before I can remove this. Lean back against Nicky for me." Damon was talking to her softly and gently. Nick, however, couldn't speak at all.

They'd wanted to carry her down to the offices once Damon had seen the wound, but she screamed as soon as he lifted her again. Her eyes were glazed with pain and he couldn't make her scream again. The sound ripped through his heart. The glass had gone straight through her shoe, as he had first seen and it was still bleeding. She had told him when he'd gotten his heart out of his throat that she'd dropped a glass last night and had thought she'd gotten it all cleaned up. Then when she'd been rushing around today, she'd stepped onto it and it was in her foot before she knew it.

"I do not want to lean back against Nicky, nor are you going to numb my foot. If you do that, then I won't be able to walk, and I have to be to work in an hour. Just rip the fucking thing out so I can glue it shut and we can all be on our merry way." She was crying again. Nick wasn't sure why, but he wanted to punch someone for it.

"There isn't any work you can't put off until Monday, if then. I don't want you in the offices, now shut up and let him numb you." Nick reached out to pull her against his chest to steady her, and she slapped his hands away.

"I'm not working for you tonight, you jackass. I have to go to Mick's and work. And I am going; I need the money. Surely one of you three men can pull that out, can't you? Please just do it." Damon looked at him with a frown. He didn't know who Mick was either and started to say something.

"You work at Big Mick's? Cool, are you a stripper? 'Cause I gotta tell you, if you are then..." Nick only took a step toward Byron. Just one, and he shut up.

"You are not a stripper! I won't have it. And why do you need the money? Am I not paying you enough? I would think that the way you live, rent free, you'd have more than..."

"*Yeah, you would think that, wouldn't you*?" she screamed at him. "I can't cash those checks. I have to work to eat. Here." She reached behind her and grabbed the clipped bundle of envelopes from the front of the refrigerator and tossed them at him. They all had Grant Corporation stamped in the upper left hand corner. And all but one of them was still sealed. "I have to have a credit history to open a checking account, but I can't get a credit history because I don't have a flipping account. Without the history, I can't cash those stupid checks, and so on. I asked that dick head in accounting to give me cash and she laughed at me. Stupid bitch."

"I don't understand. You need a credit check to open a checking account. That's ridiculous. I gave you a credit card. Why didn't you just use that? Or better yet, one of those check cashing places I see ads for on the television? That would have given you cash at least."

Nick was still looking at the six pay checks. Why hadn't she said...but she had, he remembered, weeks ago. He'd told her to go to accounting to get it taken care of. He hadn't even bothered to see if she'd gotten it resolved.

"Oh yeah, that. It's in Mr. Grant's freezer. I was informed by your lovely bitch of an account that I need to have approval every time I spend over fifteen dollars and she was not going to let me spend your money willy nilly. Yes, willy nilly spender, that's me. And have you seen how much they charge to cash a check at one of those places? It would take me years to ever catch up. I knew a girl on my row in prison who was into them for thousands of … *Take. The. Fucking. Glass out now!*"

Nick looked at Byron with a raised brow and he backed up. "I don't have it. I've…she's never been to my place."

"No, that freezer. Just open it up; it's right there. Might as well take it. I can't use it either."

Nick looked back at Damon and saw that he'd pulled a syringe out and had filled it while she was talking. He nodded at him and he suddenly knew that he was going to knock her out. If they didn't, she'd be walking to the bar glass or no glass.

"Morgan, honey. You need to relax all right? Let me hold you while Damon removes the glass." She slapped at his hands again, but they weren't as hard as before. He didn't know whether it was because she was resigned to the fact that he was going to touch her, or she was getting weaker from blood loss.

"Stay away from me, I mean it. I told you before that I — *ouch!* What the hell was that?" When she tried to pull her thigh away from Damon, he held tighter. Nick knew she was going to have a bruise, but she'd left them no choice. Damon didn't look up at her as he finished the injection.

"I'm sorry, sweetheart, but I can't work with you moving around like that. You're going to go to sleep now and when you wake up, the glass will be gone and I'll have you all stitched up. You're not going to be walking on that foot for awhile, but we'll take care of you." Damon pulled out the syringe and began rubbing the area while Nick held her hands away. He could feel when the drugs started to kick in; she was fighting less and relaxing more.

"I hate you, both of you. And I quit. I won't work...you tricked me...I want to go back to prison. Please take me back... there has to be a way for me...I hate you..." Nick pulled her close to his chest and just held her.

The next twenty minutes were tense while Damon worked to get the glass out. It was right up against the bone and had to be worked loose before he could remove it completely. Even as out as she was, she whimpered a few times. Nick whispered nonsense in her ear and continued to hold her tight and tired not to think about her telling him she hated him. He watched Damon put in every one of the fifty-six stitches on the bottom of her foot, then the twenty-three on the top; he felt every pull of the thread, every stick of the needle.

"Now what do we do with her? Because I got a feeling if we don't do something with her, she'll be on her way to Mick's as soon as she wakes up." Byron had a point.

"We take her with us. Mom wanted her there anyway. This way, we can keep an eye on the swelling and she won't be able to go to work. She'll have a happy Thanksgiving with us."

Nick looked at his brother and thought he was insane. Not about taking her with them, that was the only option they did have, but if he thought she was going to be happy, or thankful, then he'd eat her ugly pink bag.

"There's something else you two need to see," Byron said as he returned to the kitchen I, hummm...I went to her bedroom to get her something less...well more and...come on." He led them through the bedroom and into the bathroom.

Nick laid her down on the bed. She had to have clean clothes and she was not wearing what she had on in public, although if she wanted to wear it to the office for him sometime, he wouldn't... *Whoa! Stop right there, bucko!*

Nick looked down at her clothes. The shirt was a black sleeveless half shirt that had *Mick's* written across her breasts in sparkly script. She had on a bra; he'd seen it several times when she'd tried to slap him away. He was intrigued with the little ladybugs that danced along the cups of it. Her belly was bare from the bottom of the skimpy shirt to the top of her micro skirt. Her skirt was also black, and very, very short. She had on thigh-high stockings that were a good inch below the skirt itself and left the creamy inch of skin exposed. He found himself wanting to lick the area and wanting to cover it up. Licking it was winning, hands down. He reluctantly left her laying there and went into the bathroom. But not before he pulled a sheet from the bottom of the bed and gently covered her up.

"Ah, hell. She never left prison at all, did she?" he said as he entered the room behind Damon.

CHAPTER SEVENTEEN

They were driving home and Nick was thinking about the woman in his arms. She was a quandary to him. She could speak several languages, run his office with an iron fist, and work two jobs without missing a beat. She also inspired loyalty in others toward her that amazed him beyond words. His mother, for one, and then her other boss, Mick Sugar. He grinned when he thought about that conversation.

Nick had to call Mick's and tell them that she'd wouldn't be in tonight, or probably for the rest of the week. The man, while surly at first, nearly took Nick's head off when he told him she was injured and that was why she couldn't come in. He had demanded that he be kept up to date on her progress and told that her job was safe as long as she wanted it.

"Yes, sir. My brothers and I are taking her to our family home to care for her there. My brother Damon is a doctor and he'll be keeping a close eye on her." He felt as if he was explaining why he'd taken the last cookie to his father rather than calling someone off for work.

"You got a chaperone up there? You ain't taking her up there for any illicit activities, are you? I want you to know that I was a Green Beret in my time, and I'll kill you so slowly and painfully you'll wish for death." Nick believed him. In that moment, he believed he would actually do it.

"No, sir! My...our mother and step-father are there too. No sir, we all are going to care for her like she's our own flesh and blood. I swear."

Nick had turned around when he heard Byron snort. Glaring at him had only made him laugh so he'd turned his back on him. He'd hung up after giving the man his mom's phone number so that he could call for himself when he wanted to check on her.

Nick glanced up at his brothers, who were deep in conversation, and then leaned down and brushed his lips across hers. They were as soft as he thought they'd be. As much as he didn't want to, he'd fallen for the girl. He wasn't in love with her, but definitely in lust for her.

The clothes she'd had on earlier notwithstanding, it was everything about her. The color of her hair all the way down to those sexy little feet she had. He wasn't sure what he was going to do about her now that he'd notice her either.

When they pulled in the long drive to the family estate, he was resigned to the fact that he had fucked up royally with her. He wondered, not for the first time, how he was planning to fix it. Maybe, just maybe, he thought, she wasn't at all like his wife had been.

~~~

Morgan opened her eyes and looked around carefully. It was always a good idea to get the lay of the land, so to speak, before others knew you were awake. She'd learned this lesson the hard way.

The room she was in was beautiful, what she could see of it. There was a small lamp lit across the room so she rolled over toward it and froze.

Standing just next to the bed was a little girl. She was dressed in Pooh jammies and was holding a doll in one hand and sucking the thumb of the other. Morgan blinked several times to be sure she wasn't dreaming. While the room wasn't one she'd ever been in before, this child was way scarier in that she didn't know any kids.

"Hello. Who are you?" Morgan tried to sit up, but moaned when the pain from her foot shot up her leg and made her remember what had happened.

Morgan watched as the little girl set her doll gently on the floor and, taking her thumb out of its safe haven, she began moving her hands in sign language.

"Ah, Meggie. Hello, Meggie, I'm Morgan Becky. I'm glad to meet you."

Morgan answered her in the same way. She had learned ASL while in prison. One of the inmates had taught it to her one week. She watched her closely. She was a pretty little thing, she thought, and wondered again where she was.

"Yes, I have to go to the bathroom. Can you tell me where I am? I went to sleep at Mr. Grant's apartment and I don't remember getting here." She watched Meggie walk across the room and pick up a pair of crutches and bring them back to her. Then she pointed to a note on the bed stand.

Ms. Becky,

Don't get up without calling one of us to help you. You are to stay off that foot or else. I am just down the hall and Damon and the others are close as well. Just dial four to reach me.

Nickolas Grant

Arrogant bastard, she thought, but did not say it out loud. She asked Meggie if she knew who Nick was, and was told he was her uncle. Her father was Spencer Grant, a school teacher.

"Where's your mother?" she asked as she worked her way to

the side of the bed. And was surprised to hear that the little girl was visiting her dad for the holidays. Her mom was on another honeymoon. Her fourth. Meggie told her that she was five and got to go to school next fall.

Morgan made it to the bathroom and peed. Then finding her things on the counter, decided she probably had just enough energy to brush her teeth and wash her face. She was exhausted by the time she made it back to the bed.

"Well, kid, I'm worn out. Why don't you go to bed and I'll see you before I leave in the morning, okay?" She watched in astonishment as Meggie went to the other side of the bed and crawled in with her doll and thumb. Morgan was too tired to argue. Besides, what harm could it do? She got in with her.

CHAPTER EIGHTEEN

The house was in a tizzy. Meggie was gone. The nursemaid had come tearing out of the little girl's room about an hour ago screaming that she'd been kidnapped, stolen by aliens, and had run away all in one breath. It had taken Spencer ten minutes to calm her down.

"What happened to her, do you think? I've searched everywhere I can think of. Christ!" Spencer was pacing and, frankly, driving the household crazy.

"She ever run away before? I mean, with you?" She'd taken off a couple times from her mother over the past few weeks, and everyone was concerned about the reason for that. Nick thought it was because her mother was a bitch, but he kept that opinion to himself.

"No, especially not here. She loves coming here with Mom and Dan. I'm going to take a walk around the grounds again, maybe look in the..."

Nick turned to see what had stopped him. Coming down the stairs was Meggie and Morgan. Meggie was clutching her dolly while she waited for Morgan to move slowly down the steps. The progress was made slower because she would stop to move the crutches out of the way and "talk" with her at every step.

Spencer ran to his daughter and scooped her up in his arms.

He was raining kisses all over her face and holding her to him as he turned to Morgan.

"How did you find her?" Even from across the room, Nick could see the look of confusion on her face. Evidently, so did Spence. "She's been missing, and I thought she'd...never mind. Where did you find her?" Spencer asked Morgan.

"I didn't, she found me. She came into the bedroom around two I guess. She was just there when I opened my eyes. She's been very helpful to me already, haven't you?" Nick watched her answer his brother in both voice and sign language so that Meggie could keep up. "I'm all packed, so I'd really like to go back to the Grant building now."

"Hello, Morgan, welcome to my home. You're staying for Thanksgiving dinner, honey. Didn't these idiots tell you?" Ms. Parker came out of the kitchen just as Morgan got to the bottom of the stairs.

"No, they didn't. But I'm not staying. I...if I could use your phone, I'll call someone to come and get me. I didn't realize it was Thanksgiving." She turned to glare at Nick then she moved to follow his mom in the kitchen. He followed as well.

"You are not going back home. It's home, not the Grant building, not Byron's apartment, home. Why do you have such a problem with that? Home, four letters. Shouldn't be too hard to remember for someone with your obvious intellect."

"Well, I can think of another four letters that go very nicely with 'off' that I'm betting you're very familiar with too. Would you like to know what they are? Ms. Parker, I really need to use the phone, please." When she turned her back on him, he saw red. Damn it, he'd had about enough of her.

"You are not going home. You are going to stay and have an enjoyable dinner with us. Then on Sunday night, if I don't murder you between now and then, I'll take you back to your apartment. Sit down before you fall." She was swaying slightly. Didn't the stupid woman know when to take it easy?

Morgan sat down and, before he could feel any sort of satisfaction for it, she swung at him with her crutch, knocking both his feet out from under him. He landed hard on his ass and hands.

"Fuck! That hurt. What the hell do...?"

"Listen to me, you arrogant jackass. I do not take orders from you. I am going back to the fucking Grant building and staying in the fucking apartment that you ordered me into. Then, on Monday morning, if I haven't killed *you* before then, I will collect my last check and quit. *I hate you!*" And before he could say a single word, she burst into tears.

CHAPTER NINETEEN

Morgan watched the two young boys play the video game on the big television. Friggin' huge would be a better description, she thought with a smile. They were trying to be quiet, they really were, but they were having fun.

"I did not lure you in there. You went on your own. Do you see me having a string around your neck? I don't think so. You're dead because you're stupid." The bigger boy was still alive, much to the consternation of the little guy.

"I'm not stupid, and I'm telling Dad. You ain't supposed to call people stupid anymore. It makes you sound illi...ilit...stupid."

"I think you mean illiterate. And he's correct; you aren't stupid. The true definition of stupid is lacking normal intelligence or understanding, or slow-witted. You don't seem to be either of those. I think the word you're looking for is ignorant. It implies a lack of knowledge, either generally, or on some particular subject, such as this game for instance." She flushed. She hadn't meant to speak out loud, but now she had their full attention. "Sorry. Ignore me."

"Gee, lady, you sound like a dictionary or something." The younger one set down his controller on the table and walked back to where she was lying on the couch.

Damon had made her come in here earlier this morning so

that he could change the bandage and have a look at her foot. He said that it was swelling quite a bit, and wanted her to sit with it elevated. He'd also given her something for the pain, which had knocked her out again. She didn't know what time it was, but she thought she'd been asleep for some time.

"My name is Jacob Parker. That's my brother James. Dan Parker is our grandda. Uncle Damon said your name was Morgan Becky and that we were to leave you be and try and keep it down to a dull roar if we could." He grinned at her and, just like that, she fell in love with him.

Jacob was a handsome little guy. He told her he was seven and his brother, nine, almost ten. They were both blond and blue-eyed and loved to fight with each other.

"Wanna play with us? We have lots of controllers and I can show you how if you wanna." James had obviously died or given up and had come over to join them on the couch. "I can help you over to the television with your sore foot and all."

"I don't know how to play at all. I mean, I've never played video games before. So why don't I just watch you two play? But I would like to sit closer." She was amazed at the size of the set and wanted to see if the picture looked as good up close as it did from halfway across the room.

It took them twenty minutes to get her set up and her foot properly propped up before they were huddled around her and the controller. James was surprisingly patient with her, but she caught on fast, so that could have been some of it. Jacob suggested that she could just play on easy with them. They wouldn't kill her too much and she could learn faster that way. She agreed only because he was jumping around so much she feared he'd fall on her.

"If you push the red button, you'll reload your weapon, but

you have to hurry, 'cause you're dying. Again."

Morgan grinned at him and looked down at the thingy in her hand. The buttons didn't move around, so why did she have to look every time? She didn't know, but she was having the time of her life. When she looked up again, Nick was standing in front of the television. *Well, fuck!*

"Hey, Uncle Nick, we can't see. Move it or lose it, will ya? That's it, Aunt Morgan, kill the sucker! Die, pond scum, die!" She froze up and would have sat there for much longer if Nick hadn't nudged her a little. Jacob had just called her "aunt."

"Can I play with you?"

Morgan slowly turned to look at him and nearly swallowed her tongue. He was looking directly at her when he asked, and for some silly reason, she didn't think he was talking about the game. She blushed furiously and looked down again. *Yeah right,* she thought, *he so wants to play with you. He can barely stand to be in the same house with you, and you think ...well, so not going there.*

"Here, but you gotta wait until James dies. Aunt Morgan is always dead first, but she is lasting longer than two minutes now. She's doing good — for a girl." He winked at her, the cheeky little kid.

"I lasted longer than you in the last campaign, kiddo. And I had a higher kill ratio to time alive than both of you two games ago." *So there,* she thought.

"Yeah, but it doesn't really say much when you're only alive for three minutes and you start blasting the second you start. She killed two of her own men in that one too, Uncle Nick. Then she made this girly noise like she'd really hurt them." James restarted the game and they were setting her up again.

Morgan tried to scoot over when Nick sat down next to her, but the pillow stool arrangement for her foot made it nearly impossible for her to get over too far. She huffed at him and he had the nerve to smile at her.

"I'll be on Morgan's team and you two play against us this time. I'm better at this, but I have Aunt Morgan, so how much of a handicap do I get?"

The negotiation went on for another few minutes, but she tuned them out. Her foot was beginning to hurt again, and she was in need of a bathroom break and maybe something to eat. The whole house smelled really good. She rolled over to her hands and knees to get up when she was suddenly standing up with Nick helping her. In the next second, she was scooped up in his arms.

"Put me down, you idiot! I'm too heavy and I have on a dress. I don't..." She was frantically trying to put it back down around her thighs and not be dropped at the same time.

"Yeah, I know you don't like to be touched. I'm taking you to the bathroom, if that's where you were headed, and then I'll bring you back. Be quiet and stop squirming around." She had to put her arm around his neck to hold on and she when she felt his muscles under her hand flex, she jerked it back to her lap.

They made it to the downstairs powder room and when he put her down, she was suddenly turned around to face him. He kissed her quickly on the mouth and turned her back around. "I'll be right out here when you're done," was all he said as she hobbled inside.

CHAPTER TWENTY

Morgan stood there for several minutes just staring at the wallpaper. It was pretty, she thought, mauve flowers with tiny little blue and pink buds. *He kissed me.* There were pictures on the wall of what appeared to be family members. One looked like it could be Damon and Spencer as small boys. *He kissed me on the mouth.* She'd never seen a toilet that was any other color than white, but both it and the sink were a deep mauve. The light fixtures had the same pattern of flowers wrapped around the glass domes that covered the blub. *Right on her lips, he kissed me.*

Morgan realized that she had been standing there leaning against the counter for too long when she heard a voice. It sounded like Mr. Parker asking Nick if everything was all right.

"Yeah, Morgan just needed to go to the bathroom. I'm waiting to take her back. I think maybe she might be hungry though."

There was a mumbled response, but she had turned on the tap to cover the noise of her going to the bathroom. Moving slowly so she didn't bump her foot, she stood up to wash her hands and then dry them. She had just turned off the water when there was a short knock at the door.

"Almost finished. I'll be out in a sec." Morgan ran her fingers through her hair and started to reach for the knob.

"Morgan, will you let me in, please?" It was Nick—Dr. Grant.

She turned the little tab and then opened the door to come out. He shouldered his way in before she took a step.

"I...I'm finished. I was just..." His mouth covered hers and cut off her sentence, her breathing, and her thought process.

Nick pulled her closer to him as she shifted around so that she was resting on the counter. With a slight lift of her bottom, he lifted her injured foot by her calf and wrapped it around his hip as he stepped between her legs.

"Morgan, give me your mouth. I want to taste you, please?" She felt his tongue trace the seam of her lips and she opened them slightly. His tongue swept inside and tangled with hers. She felt his groan rumble through his chest and his hands tightened on her hips.

Morgan pulled back slightly and heard him growl before he allowed her to pull back further to look up at him.

"What...you kissed me. You can't just...I'm mad at you. I don't want you to kiss me."

Of course, that would have been much more believable if she didn't currently have her ankles hooked around his hips, she thought with a grimace. Apparently, he thought so too, because he grinned in response and kissed her again, a short but no less heated one this time.

"I can tell. And you do mad very well." With another grin, he scooped her up into his arms and waited by the closed door until she turned the handle so they could exit. She was really getting tired of being picked up all the time. By the time she felt like she could say something to him about being mad at him, he was putting her down in a kitchen chair where all the women seemed to have gathered.

"Mom, I think Morgan could use some lunch. I know I can." He ruffled Jacob's hair and kissed his mother on her cheek. He

Kathi S. Barton

started introducing Morgan to his aunts.

"Aunt Pea, Aunt Mary, this is Morgan Becky. She works for me and is our guest. Morgan, these are my aunts Peabody and Mary, my mom's sisters. Their husbands, Thomas and Mike, respectively are in the living room with Dan watching football. My two cousins, Tom and Janie, are Aunt Pea's kids; they're watching the game as well. You've not met my brothers Jamie or Devin, but they're in there too, I think. I am a man on a mission and have come to rescue and feed my poor injured damsel in distress." She knew she was looking at him oddly, but she couldn't help it.

"Who are you, and what have you done with Nickolas Grant, the guy with the rod for a spine and a pain in my ass?" It was out before she could stop it. Startled with herself, she looked around the room.

His Aunt Pea was bright red with tears streaming down her cheeks and her hand clamped tight over her mouth. Ms. Parker was staring at her with her mouth opened and mirth evident in her bright eyes. But his Aunt Mary was gulping in large gulps of air and braying with laughter. It wasn't long before the other aunt was hysterical too. Ms. Parker finally gave in and had to be lead to a chair to try and gain control of herself. These people were nuts, Morgan thought. Certifiably.

It wasn't long before the boys were back with the other members of the household and regaling the story for them. When Morgan chanced a glance at Dr. Grant, she knew the true meaning of payback if his look was any indication. And, oh boy, he was going to make her pay.

Morgan watched as he stalked toward her from across the room. She looked around desperately for a way to escape, but there was nowhere to go. Standing up and hanging onto the table, she started moving toward the little door to the right of the sink. Almost there, she felt him snake his arm around her waist seconds before he brought his mouth to her ear.

"I think not." She felt his breath hot against her neck, his lips moving along the shell of her ear. Had he not pulled back when he did, she was sure she would have leaned back into his chest and...she didn't know what, but he felt so good.

"Let me go. I'm sorry I want you to let me go." Her voice sounded strange and heavy. She was nearly panting by the time he picked her up with his arm around her and turned her to face the room. They were still laughing when he started nuzzling her neck, nipping at her tender skin. Before she could stop herself, she was leaning into his embrace and turned to his mouth with hers. "Please...?"

This kiss was different, it was...hungry. She was hungry for his mouth, his taste. She was barely aware of him turning her in his arms and tightening his hold on her, less aware of them backing into the room where she'd been headed. The other people in the room disappeared with the closing of the door, the world gone with the flick of the lock.

CHAPTER TWENTY-ONE

"Morgan, oh baby." She was pressed against the wall with her legs wrapped around him again when she felt his cock hard against her. She had a few seconds of terror, but he touched her breast tenderly and ran his tongue along the curve of her ear and she felt suddenly...safe. But they couldn't, shouldn't, do this. She was sure there was a good reason, and as soon as he stopped touching her, she'd remember what it was.

"I...I don't know...this...this shouldn't be happening. Nickolas, you don't want to do this, I'm...please...yes, no! Nick, stop now... oh yes, please." She couldn't seem to make up her mind. Well, that wasn't quite true. Her mind and body knew exactly what they wanted. It was her mouth that kept trying to regain control.

"I want you. I want you now, Morgan." She felt the cool, air conditioned air hum across her bared breast seconds before he laved it with his tongue. Her nipple tightened and puckered hard against the roof of his mouth, the combination of his hot, wet tongue and the vent making her ache with need. Her body's reaction to that was to arch into him.

Long ago, she thought she'd never want a man to ever touch her again. Never want to feel one touch her in anyway whatsoever, for his body to come over her, into her. Now, right now, she knew that she wanted Nickolas with a desperation that she'd never felt before, nor would ever again.

Reaching between them, she cupped him, his cock against her hand. When he pressed harder against her and suckled on her nipple, she felt the stirrings of her first climax. Tightening her legs, using the wall as a brace, she moved up around him. Their mutual groans of approval ran down along their skin and throughout their bodies.

"Nick! Nick, open the door! We need to get in there." She stiffened, as did he. Morgan wanted to snarl at the man on the other side of the door, but froze in horror. What were they doing?

"Just a...give me, us, a minute," he yelled at the unseen man. He laid his head against her breast and she whimpered when his breath moved across the now sensitive nipple. He was shaking and it took her a few seconds to realize he was laughing.

"This is not funny, you jackass. Let me down. I can't believe... where are we? You know, I don't care. I want out of here, and don't you dare touch..." His mouth was on hers again and she moaned again as his tongue swept against hers. Damn it, what was wrong with her? She was acting like a cat in heat.

When he pulled his mouth away, he moved to her ear again. "I want you. And if Devin hadn't interrupted us, I'd be deep inside you right now and we both know it. I didn't intend for this to happen...well, yeah I did, but not in the pantry of my parents' home." She watched as he gently pulled her blouse back down. "Morgan, we're going to have to walk out of here and they are going to all be there, if I know them. Our best bet to get through this is to ignore them, all right?" Nick moved her gently away from him and started to pull her top back down, but brushed his knuckles across her nipple first. She arched into his touch. "Ah, baby, this isn't easy for me." Quickly, he stepped back to re-snap his jeans. She hadn't even realized they'd gone that far.

When they entered the kitchen, with her once again in his arms, the room was empty. Moving along the hall, they went back into the room where the large TV was, and he sat her down on the couch. With a quick kiss and a "be right back," she was alone in the big room.

Morgan laid her head down on her hands. She had nearly had sex with him, her boss, in the pantry of his family home. Were there even names for this kind of conduct? Oh yeah, it was called stupidity.

Morgan jerked her head up when someone touched her arm. Meggie was standing there beside her with doll and thumb. Morgan smiled at her, and pulled her up into her lap to give and receive a hug.

"Hello, angel, how are you today?" The two of them conversed for several minutes before Nick came back into the room with a plate and a glass. He set the plate on the little side table next to the couch and handed her the glass of tea.

"Hey there, baby. How are my favorite girls doing?" He kissed his niece on the head and sat down next to Morgan.

Morgan explained how Meggie wanted her to braid her hair back and asked him if Spencer would mind.

"No, he'd probably be grateful for the help. He's told me on several occasions that he'd rather have his toenails pulled out than try and fix up her hair." Meggie's long hair was thick and curly just like Morgan's, with the exception of the color.

Morgan didn't have a lot of experience with kids, actually none at all if you didn't count the kids in the home with her. She turned the little girl around and began combing the long tresses with the pink comb Meggie had brought to Morgan. It took her about thirty minutes to get it in a reasonable order, and then she began pulling the four strains together into a thick plat. When she reached the end, she wrapped a band around the bottom and tied the bright, lemon-colored ribbon around it. The second ribbon of the same color, she tied around her thumb.

"This will be much prettier than it sticking out of your mouth, don't you think? I like it." She kissed the tip of Meggie's thumb and let her slip off her lap.

Morgan realized how tired she was and how badly her foot was thumping about ten minutes later when Jacob and James came back in to resume their game. She didn't play much this time; her concentration was crap. She had made the mistake, or not, of running her tongue across her lips and tasted him. Heat built inside of her again. She could almost feel his body pressed against hers. What the hell was wrong with her?

CHAPTER TWENTY-TWO

"Aunt Morgan, I was...can you help...I know you're not really my aunt and all, but I was wondering if you could help me. You see, I gotta do this report on my hero. And I gotta have it done by Christmas, but I ain't having any luck. I can do the stuff. You know, the writing and all, but not the research."

Jacob had flopped down beside her not long after she'd asked Damon for something for the pain. She was beginning to feel woozy, but not completely out of it yet. It was probably why she agreed to such a stupid idea.

Morgan would help him out by looking up as much information as she could find on the Internet, and print it up for him. His hero, of all people, was his Uncle Nick, so she "should have lots of insider stuff on him," he had said. When she had blushed at his comment, he must have assumed she was hot because he had started fanning her with a magazine from the table.

"All you gotta do is Google him. I'm sure there's tons of stuff on him. He's, like, famous and all. I really wanna make a good grade on this. He'll have-a come to my school and have a lunch with me if I can win." It was the eyes that got her. Big and brown, he'd put just enough sadness in them to reel her in. Damned drugs didn't help either.

He loaned her his laptop and showed her how to find the house printer; there were apparently several to print to. He had also given her as much background information he had, like birthday, address, and his full name to help with the search. He was really good about it; he didn't play anymore games, but sat and helped her decide what he wanted to use in his report. Before long, it was dinner.

Morgan hadn't planned on eating with them; she wasn't a part of either blended family, nor had she come there as a guest. When everyone got up to go to the formal dining room, she stayed in the game room and kept looking things up for Jacob.

"Morgan, you're holding up dinner. You want me to help you?" Spencer had come into the room not two minutes after they'd just left.

"Holding it up, I don't understand. Did you need me to serve or something? I'm not sure how much I can help out, but I should have assumed that... Yes, let me get up. I'm truly sorry. I just took a pain pill."

Morgan was babbling. She knew it and so did he. She was embarrassed and hated feeling that way. As she struggled to get up quickly, she bumped her foot and cried out with the pain.

"Morgan, it's okay, honey. Come on, we want you to eat with us, not serve us. What a silly notion. Just take a deep breath, that's it. The pain should subside soon, and then I'll carry you in, all right?" He was sitting on the table in front of the couch when Nick walked in.

"Spence, what's going on?" Morgan looked up at him when he spoke and blushed again. She was trying to tell Spencer that she'd rather not eat with them, would in fact feel much better serving them instead.

"You're girlfriend thinks I want her to come serve us. I was just explaining.."

"I'm not his girlfriend! I'm just...I work for him, nothing more. I...you've got it all wrong, I don't, I'm not...you're wrong. I'm not family. I'll just finish the sandwich in here. Alone."

Morgan didn't look at either man as she set the computer aside and picked up the little plate from earlier. When she was suddenly picked up, the plate and food on it went flying. When she began to slip from his arms, Nick tightened his grip and held her closer to his body. She frantically looked around and saw that Spencer had left the room.

"Morgan, look at me." She didn't, but looked everywhere else she could. This was so mortifying, and she wanted to go back to Byron's apartment.

"Please put me down, Dr. Gra...what the hell are you doing?" She was suddenly back down on the couch and he was on top of her. Before she could move out from under him, he was kissing her again. Damn, this man could kiss, she thought.

"Do you feel me against you?" He pressed himself hard into her and pulled her hands up over her head. The terror hit her full force. She was back in the basement with those men raping her.

"Please, don't hurt me. Please, please, please..." she whispered desperately.

Her body, drenched in a sudden sweat, began to fight against the weight. She was no longer in the Parker home, but the home of Randall Bennett. She wasn't in the game room any longer, but cuffed to the cot in the basement. She wasn't being held in the arms of a man who had kissed her earlier, but of the men who would take their turn with her body. The screams ripped from her, over and over. The voices yelling at her had no meaning. She was no longer safe, no longer free. The pain in her arm barely registered, and then everything went black.

CHAPTER TWENTY-THREE

Morgan woke up on a bed. There was a small body tucked tight against her side. Meggie. When she tried to move out from under her, the little girl tightened her hold around her arm.

"She insisted on sleeping with you. She said that you'd need her when you woke up. I think she's worried about you." The whispered voice was coming from across the room. She couldn't make out who it was, but it was not Nickolas.

"I...someone sedated me. I...where am I?" She started to move to the other side and encountered another body, this one considerably bigger and male. Nickolas was in bed with her.

"Yes, my brother Damon did. You were...you'd had a fright. I'm Devin Grant, by the way. We didn't get a chance to meet earlier. I'm sorry about that. My family is downstairs and as soon as you feel like you can, they'd like for you to come down. Nicky hasn't been there long; he feels bad for scaring you. Can you? Get up, I mean." They were going to make her leave.

Morgan didn't blame them. They'd been ready to sit down to their Thanksgiving dinner. She'd lost control, screaming like an idiot and ruining their dinner. No, she thought, she didn't blame them.

"I need my bag before I leave. It has my stuff in it; it's pink. You can't miss it. I'm really sorry about dinner. I...it wasn't Dr. Grant's fault. I got...I have nightmares, you see. Well, that's not true; I have them even when I'm awake. Tell him…tell him it's nothing to do with him. I just, sometimes I get a...can I go now?" There was no excuse for what she'd done and she knew it.

"Are you finished? And I swear, Morgan, if you call me Dr. Grant one more time I'm going to paddle you but good I've had your nip…" She heard Nickolas take a deep breath, the hot air moving along her neck. "Devin, why don't you take Meggie down the hall? Morgan and I'll be a few more minutes." She started to scramble to the other side, the side that Meggie had been sleeping, when Nickolas hauled her back with an arm around her waist.

"Let me go. I want to go back to Mr. Grant's apartment. Why you brought me here is... Why did you bring me here? Never mind, I want—"

"Does it bother you when I'm on top of you, or was it me pulling your arms up too?" He was so matter-of-fact that she just answered.

"Both, but mostly my arms. I...he tied me to the bed and I couldn't... I don't like to be touched, restrained like that. I need you to let me go."

"No, not yet. What if I kissed you now, like this? Would it scare you if I kissed you with you beneath me? Does it remind you of them?" No one had asked her before. Of course, no one had been this close to her before either.

"I...they never kissed. I'd never been kissed until you. I think if you let me up, I could have Mick…"

"They didn't kiss you? And no, Mick isn't coming to get you. Just hush and answer my questions. How could you have never been kissed before? With a mouth like yours...and I don't mean the smart-assed part, but the taste of you."

Morgan glared up at him. He had thrown his left leg across her hips and then tucked it around her. He was just too heavy to move without his help, or cooperation.

"The first guy who tried, I bit through his lip until I got blood. They didn't take the gag off after that. It could also have had something to do with my screaming. And I am not a smart ass. Get off me, you big dick head. I...your family's waiting on you down — ouch! That fucking hurt."

Nick had swatted her across the butt, hard. Then he rubbed the area with his hand until it wasn't a rub anymore, but a caress. Then it became a pull. He was pulling her closer to him, his body. And she wanted it.

Nick didn't press her into the bed like she was afraid he'd do. But pulled her on top of him as he shifted to his back. Mindful of her foot, he spread her legs wide across his hips, across his groin. Still pulling her toward him, he gripped her hips and pulled her harder, down against him.

"Nickolas...I ..."

Nick sat up and covered her mouth with his, devouring her, savoring her. She moaned against his mouth and then again when he began making his way down her throat to her collar bone, then lower, his lips leaving a trail of wet, hot nips and bites. He brought his hands up from her hips and cupped both of her breasts in his palms and lifted them high, high into his mouth. When he bit her nipple through her clothing, she surged hard into him, wrapped both her hands around his head, and pulled him closer to her.

"Come for me, Morgan. Ride me until you come apart. Come against me like this. Now, baby, come now." Lifting her shirt and yanking her bra away from what he wanted, he took her hard peak into his mouth and suckled, hard and deep into his hot mouth.

Morgan felt it building, her need nearly out of control. She was riding him, the friction of his cock pressing against her mound pushing her harder and faster to what they both wanted. When she felt him nibble on her flesh and take her into his mouth again, she came apart. Had he not kissed her at the moment, the entire house would have heard her scream out her release. Over and over, her body convulsed and jerked. He held her close to him, whispering into her ear as she settled. When she finally laid lax over him, he lifted her chin to look at her.

"We're going downstairs now to have dinner. I don't want to. I want to bury myself deep, deep inside of you and have you come like that over me, onto my cock. And I want to come inside of you. I don't want to leave this bed again until we've both had our fill of each other, but they're waiting for us. Then after dinner, I'm going to bring you up here and we are going to pick up right here, understand?"

Morgan could only nod at him. He'd given her pleasure and had taken none for himself. And, boy oh boy, had she gotten pleasure, she thought with a sloppy smile. Even now she wanted to ride him again until he could feel this good and she could again.

"If you keep looking at me like that, we aren't going anywhere." She watched as he slipped out of bed and went to the adjoining bathroom. She could see his cock pressed hard against his pants. She wanted to touch him, to feel him in her hands, in her body. She moaned aloud and he growled at her. "Get up before you can't. I mean it, Morgan. If you keep this up, you won't leave this room for a month." As he entered the bathroom and shut the door, she wondered if he actually thought that was a punishment. When she heard him flick the lock, she burst out laughing.

CHAPTER TWENTY-FOUR

They were all around the table when he carried her downstairs. Devin had told everyone that she was awake, and they gathered together to wait. The table was beautiful and full of more food than Morgan had seen in a year.

"How are you feeling, sweetheart? You look better; there's color in your cheeks."

Morgan stared open mouthed at Ms. Parker, and would have continued staring if Nickolas had not reached over and closed her mouth.

"No, baby, she doesn't know what we've been up to. But I would say the others do. Just ignore them and enjoy your meal. You're going to need the extra calories before this night is over."

Morgan felt a blush race over her body, and then she heard Byron snicker and blushed harder. With a very heartfelt glare from her, he settled down and started filling his plate. The other man, she thought it must be Jamie, just laughed harder when she tried the same on him. The whole family was full of men who were full of themselves, she thought.

"Whose turn is it to watch the parade this year?" Damon had asked as they settled in the largest living room Morgan had ever seen after dinner.

Morgan had picked up her crutches to use, but found that her foot really hurt, and was carried by Nick again. She was either going to have to get better soon, or lose some serious weight. When she said as much to Nickolas, he growled at her. She didn't know why, but she was really getting to like that sound coming from him.

"I think its Dan's turn this year. Devin had it last year. Too bad, old man. I was buying lunch at Mario's this year." Spencer patted him hard on the back as he grinned at the other man.

"Every year since Meggie was born, one of us stays home with her. We record the Macy's parade and watch it with her while the others shop. The next person on the list buys lunch for us all. It's a lot of fun," Nickolas explained when she asked.

"I can watch her. I mean, if Dr. Grant doesn't mind leaving her with me. I'll be here anyway, and there isn't any reason for someone to stay if I don't shop."

Morgan had said it before she'd thought. She should have cleared it with Spencer before putting him on the spot like that. Besides, she hadn't been invited anyway.

"Really? You'd watch her. I mean, she really likes you already. And her hair, I meant to tell you earlier, it's beautiful. Plus, the ribbon on her thumb has worked too. She won't take it off."

At the curious looks, he explained how Morgan had tied a ribbon, a bow, around Meggie's thumb and told her it was prettier this way instead of in her mouth. She hadn't sucked on it since.

"Oh, that's just lovely! And it worked too? Congratulations, my dear, you accomplished in one day what countless doctors haven't been able to do in months." Mrs. Parker sounded genuinely happy.

Morgan flushed. It had been years since anyone had

complimented her, and here she was getting it twice in one day.

After a little while, Jacob asked for her help and she made her way into the gaming room. She thought that he wanted her to start on his project, but he actually wanted her to be his partner in another game.

"You do all right for a girl. Besides, I get a handicap when I play with you." He grinned at her and they both laughed.

Jacob had brought her in the laptop and every time she died, which was taking longer and longer to happen, she'd research a little more. It was kinda fun.

While she was in prison, she'd taken a few classes on web design and set up. She'd gotten so good at it that she was able to make a few sites for some of the guards and their wives. One was a site she set up was for an interior designer and she told Morgan that her business had tripled since it was put online. It was getting fairly late and she was just printing up the last of the pages when Nick came into the room. He had her papers in his hand.

CHAPTER
TWENTY-FIVE

Nick had been sitting in the office looking up some last minute investments when the printer behind him started printing. He didn't really think much about it until it signaled it was out of paper and he'd turned around to refill it. There were about twenty sheets already there so he set them on the corner of his desk and filled it up. His name caught his eye as he turned back around and looked at the sheets closer. They were about him.

Someone was doing research on him, extensive research, it seemed. He looked at the ones printed, then picked up the last sheets as they came out. All thirty-nine pages were about him, from his childhood all the way until last week when he'd gone to the charity thing with his brother. He gathered them all up and went to see who it was.

Nick found Morgan still in the gaming room with a laptop on the table in front of her. She was the only one up.

"I found these. They were printing and it ran out of paper. Do they belong to you?" He didn't hand them to her, but stood in the doorway holding them.

"Yes, hummm, do you think I could have them please? They're not...I was doing some research on something." She didn't say anything more, but held out her hand.

Nick wanted to demand to know what she was doing. Why she was looking up things about him, but he felt he already knew the answer to that. What did every woman want when they had a very wealthy man sniffing around? Money. He had to hand it to her. She was certainly doing her homework. He handed them to her and sat in the chair across from her. His entire body was cold. He'd thought she was different. But she was really no different than any other woman he knew, especially his wife. She'd only married him for his money, his security. That's what she'd told him the day before she died.

Well, he wasn't going to be suckered in this time. No way was he letting another woman sink her claws into him. Or his family.

"Are you all right, Nickolas? You look a little..."

"Yes. I'm fine, better than fine. Are you ready for bed?" He didn't let her finish. He didn't want to hear her fake kindness right now. He wanted...he wanted her to pay.

He bent over and picked her up. When she protested again, he nearly snarled at her to drop the innocent act, that he knew what she was up to.

"You aren't heavy. Not in the slightest." He carried her up to his room and laid her on the bed. Before she could say anything, he was kissing her. It was several seconds before he realized he was scaring her, hurting her, and he backed off a little.

"I'm sorry, you're just so beautiful. I forget myself." He kissed her this time, gently, and began to unbutton her shirt as he did. She really was beautiful and sexy. It wasn't hard for him to show her his desire for her, his need.

Nick stripped her down slowly, kissing each bit of skin he revealed. Her breasts were exquisite, firm and full; her nipples were dark and the tips hard. When he took one into his mouth and suckled it, she arched against him. He continued his way down her body, removing clothing, tasting her. When she lay before him in only her panties, he stood back and stripped to his bare skin and looked at her.

"I want to be inside of you, deep inside of you." Mindful of her foot, he slowly moved to her core. Heat poured from her. Slowly, he rocked gently into her. "You're so tight, tighter than I thought you'd be," he said as he moved inside of her.

"What? What did you say?" He wanted her to know. He wanted her to know that he wasn't going to fall for her games.

"I said that you're tighter than I thought. Oh, don't worry, I'm enjoying this. But I'm not going to come. I'm not going to give you what you need to trap me." He moved again. He wanted to slam into her, take her hard and fast, but he didn't have a condom and there was no way he was coming in her.

"Trap you? What are you talking about?" She was good, he'd give her that. She had the indignant woman down pat.

"You know, into marriage, or whatever else you were researching me for. I'll fuck you, but I won't pay. Maybe we can do this some other time, when I'm more prepared. I'm willing to pay you, of course. I don't know what the going rate is for a hooker, but you'd be worth about any price. You are so tight. Did you try this on Randall? Is that what happened and you cried rape? It's not going to work with me, Morgan. You aren't going to have my bastard, and I won't let you hurt me or my family."

Nick rocked into her again and again. He couldn't seem to help himself. He needed to stop now, now before it was too late, and pulled out of her. He looked down at her and noticed that she wasn't moving, just laying there staring at him. When he got up off the bed, she rolled over and curled around herself. He hardened his heart and continued.

"I want you gone from here before I get out of the bathroom, do you hear me? And I want you to stay away from my family from now on. I don't know how you suckered my Mother into your little scheme, but you'll leave her alone too. Do you hear me?" He waited until she answered and just when he thought she wasn't going to, she said, "yes."

Nick moved to the door and looked back when he heard a sound, but didn't stop moving until he was nearly to the bathroom. He could tell she was crying, but he didn't care. Or at least, he tried not to care. He shut the door behind him and leaned against the sink.

He looked at the man in the mirror and suddenly hated him. Hated what he'd done and what he'd said. But he wasn't that man right now, and he wasn't going to be caught in a loveless marriage again. He jerked on the shower, stepped under the steaming water, and began scrubbing his skin.

CHAPTER TWENTY-SIX

Morgan heard the door click shut and her heart did too She rolled over onto her back and looked up at the ceiling. There wasn't anything going through her head other than the need to be gone. He'd said to be gone when he came out. She heard the shower turn on as she reached for her pants. When she had them up to her hips, she found her shirt and pulled it on too. Standing up, she didn't even feel the pain in her foot, didn't feel the stitches rip or the blood start to pour from the now open wound. She felt nothing, wouldn't allow herself to feel, not yet, not now.

Morgan made her way down to the kitchen. She knew there was a phone there. She wasn't up to trying to find another one. She stood there for several seconds trying to think. She didn't know where she was, didn't know whose house it was, nothing. She picked up the receiver and dialed one of the only two numbers she knew.

"This had better be fucking important to be calling me at midnight," he snarled as a way of answering.

Morgan almost hung up. Almost, but she had no other choices.

"Mr. Sugar, its Morgan. Morgan Becky. I don't...he said to be gone. I...I don't know where I am. I have to be gone, you see, and I...could you come and get me?" She started sobbing then and felt stupid and humiliated at the same time. "I'm sorry, forget it. I can...I can find my way. I'm sorry to have bothered you." She was sure he was speaking, but hung up anyway.

Morgan quietly opened the back door and slipped out into the night. When she got to the end of the drive, she looked for a mailbox and found the house number. She didn't know what good it would do her. She didn't have a phone and she still didn't know the street. She began walking toward what she hoped was town.

She didn't know how long she'd been walking when she heard the car. She ignored it just like she'd been trying to ignore the pain in her foot. But when she heard her name, she slowly turned around and tried to focus on the person. Dizziness hit her hard and she nearly fell over, would have if the person hadn't caught her.

"Christ, Morgan, why the fuck didn't you wait for me? I said I was coming. I've been—Jesus, you're bleeding, your foot..." Suddenly, she was being picked up. Mick. It was Mick.

"I don't feel so good. Could you please put me down? I have to throw up again." He either didn't hear her or didn't listen because he was still carrying her. "Please."

Mick set her down. Not on the ground where she would have preferred, but in a truck seat. A big truck, actually. And then her head was being forced between her knees.

"Just breathe, in and out, all right? What the hell happened back there that you had to leave in the middle of the night? I'm gonna kill that son of a bitch. Tell me what happened so I can tell the police why I killed him."

"I just wanna go. I don't have anywhere to go, Mr. Sugar."

And she started crying again.

"I'll take you home. My wife will kill me if I let you go anywhere else. Come on, sweetie, get inside now." He helped her inside and buckled her belt across her.

Nick had thought that she was trying to trap him. She wasn't as stupid as he thought she was. She knew what he was talking about. That's why...that's why he didn't finish. He...no baby. He didn't want her to claim...he thought she'd tried it on Randall, the man who sold her, who raped her.

Mr. Sugar took her to his house and carried her into his house where a lovely little woman was waiting for them. She had gotten one of their spare bedrooms, one of their son's, she'd said, ready, and he took her in and put her on the bed. There were bandages and clean water already there. But she was too exhausted and as soon as he laid her down, she closed her eyes and went to sleep. Her screaming woke them all up about two hours later. The nightmare was gripping her again.

CHAPTER TWENTY-SEVEN

The next time she woke up, she was in the hospital. There was an IV hooked up to her right arm and her foot was propped up high on a pillow. She felt...doped and heavy. She looked around the room and saw Mrs. Libby Sugar sitting asleep in one of the chairs in the room. About that time, a nurse came sailing into the room and woke her.

"Oh, Miss Becky, you're awake. Good. Are you hungry? The doctor said you could have something light if you wanted it. There's also something for pain if you need it."

"Doctor? I'm not...could I please have my things? I'd like to go, please." She started to sit up, but noticed that she was catheterized. She looked up at the nurse who had begun backing toward the door.

"I'll just call the doctor. He said to inform him when you woke up." She bolted so fast that Morgan didn't get a chance to stop her.

"I want to leave here. I really need to leave here. I don't have a doctor. Do you know how to remove this thingy?" She was frantic. She could hear it in Libby's voice.

"Morgan, just calm down. No one is going to hurt you. You've lost a lot of blood. When you woke up screaming the other night, we didn't know what to think. We brought you here and they contacted your doctor. Micky wasn't happy about it, but he let him treat you. They had to give you blood, you'd lost so much."

"How long have I been here? You said the other night. How long have I been here?" She was afraid. If they contacted her doctor, the only one she'd seen...

"Hello, Morgan, how are you feeling?" Damon Grant. Well, fuck.

"I want to leave. Right now. I want you to take this thing out of me so I can leave please." She was crying. Again. What if...no, she wasn't going to think about him coming in.

"He doesn't know you're here. Just me, and, well, my mom, but Nick doesn't know."

She and Damon watched Mrs. Sugar leave the room and he sat down in her chair.

"The hospital called me on Friday morning to say that a patient of mine had been admitted. I almost didn't take the call. You see, we had an emergency of our own at home. A guest had come up missing and there was blood all over the house. We didn't know what to think until Nick got up. He said that you two had had a fight and that he'd sent you to another room. He didn't know that you'd left. Is that what happened, Morgan? Did you two have a fight?"

"He told me to be gone when he came out of the bathroom." She stopped. She wasn't supposed to have anything to do with his family. That's what he'd said. "I'd like to go now, Dr. Grant. I don't want you to be my doctor anymore either. You're very nice and I'm sure you...I don't think...I'm not supposed to have you as my doctor, please. I'd like to leave right now." She looked out the window and tried to ignore the tears welling up in her eyes.

"I want you to stay a few days more. You've gotten the wound very dirty and I've had to clean it out. I've given you a tetanus shot, but I'd like to keep you at least two more days."

She couldn't look at him; she hurt so much.

"Morgan, you can talk to me. I won't tell Nick anything you say to me."

"Please." After a few more minutes, she heard him get up and leave the room. She didn't know what he was going to do. She could only hope that what he'd said was true and no one knew where she was.

A nurse came in a few minutes later and removed the catheter and handed her her bag without saying a word. Her crutches were brought in and another nurse brought in her discharge papers. After explaining that she'd need to set up an appointment with her own physician, she was free to go.

Go where, she didn't know. Mr. Sugar solved the issue by telling her that he had an apartment over the bar she could have cheap when he came in to take her there. It wasn't much, so neither was the rent, and when she was better, she'd come back to the bar to work. He also told her that Dr. Damon had gotten her things, including her money taped under the drawer, and he'd already taken it all to the apartment. He also wanted to know if she knew how to keep books, as he'd pay her for doing that while she was laid up.

~~~

Morgan had straightened out the bar's books in about three days of constant work. She knew she was overdoing it, but it was either work hard and fall in bed exhausted, or run screaming from the room. Today, she was working on a website for the bar. Not that he needed one, but she was bored and lonely.

Morgan didn't understand most of what was on the TV, and

less of the music on the radio. She usually preferred the quiet over the constant noise, but just lately she found herself craving someone, anyone, to talk to. So here she was, doing something totally useless. Well, not totally. She was getting some practice.

Morgan had found some old pictures of the bar in one of the hundreds of little cubbyholes she'd found in one of the two bedrooms. He'd told her to throw it all out, but she couldn't, not without seeing what it was. Some of the pictures were when the bar first opened about thirty years ago. It was fun to see the progression of time in the still lives. She began by scanning them with the printer and placing them in file folders by date and year. That had taken the better part of six hours. She was making a list of other things she found when her email signaled she had a message.

It was the same email address she'd had in prison, so she thought it was from someone there, and was surprised when it was from the woman she'd designed the site for who owned an interior design firm.

Ms. Becky,

I have a client that is in need of your services. He is quite the artist and has decided to expand his art to the online sales. I told him how you had worked miracles with my business, and he would like to meet you. I was hoping that we could meet for lunch this Thursday at Charlie's on Seventh Street at one o'clock. Please let me know if this is a good time for you?

Cyndi Penshaw

She could do that from here, she thought. Especially at night when the bar closed down at two o'clock. She could, at the very least, do this until she was able to get around on her foot without crutches. She wouldn't have to go out into public unless she wanted to.

The following Thursday she was making her way into the little bistro on her crutches. She'd been on them for six days now, and she thought she was getting really good on them.

Morgan saw Ms. Penshaw first, with her steel gray hair wound tightly around her head and her sparkles around her neck and wrist. Morgan had never seen anyone wear so much shiny, noisy things on her person. She was grinning until she saw who her luncheon date was. Byron Grant.

Morgan tried to turn around and go back out, but he must have seen her trying to leave. He was in front of her in a flash.

"Please don't leave, Morgan. I want to talk to you. No one knows you're here, I swear. Not even my mother. And Cyndi doesn't know anything other than I want to hire you to do some web work for me. Please stay?"

"Am I here for a job, or are you gathering intel to tell your arrogant asshole brother?" She hadn't moved to the door or the table yet.

"Yes, I need you to set me up a site, and no, I won't do intel for him. I don't care for him much right now either." She didn't move for a few moments then turned and made her way to his table. Cyndi was talking on the phone when they arrived.

"I'm sorry, I have to go. My son is sick at daycare and they won't keep him with a temperature. I need to go get him. Oh, Morgan, it is so nice to see you again. And I'm so glad you were acquitted of the horrible crime. Byron, call me next week and we'll nail down a time to fix up that shop apartment of yours." Then, she was gone.

"If you set this up like this, I'll brain you with my crutch." Morgan pulled out Cyndi's chair and propped her injured foot onto the seat.

"I swear I didn't. It worked out nicely, though, didn't it?" He had the most charming grin. She wondered if he knew that. Then she glanced around the room at the women practically drooling at him and realized, yeah, he knew it. And the effect he had on those poor, unsuspecting women too.

"I bet. I find out you set me up, there won't be a hole deep enough for you to hide in, nor a place far enough away. I know people who know people." She picked up her menu and started to read it. She was startled when he laughed loud enough that several patrons of the restaurant turned to look at them.

"Ah, Morgan, you are a card. I think I'll enjoy this merry-go-round you seem to be running around my brother. Yes, I believe I will."

Morgan didn't know what he was talking about so she chose to ignore him. For the time being anyway. After they ordered their food, she pulled out a notebook and wrote his name across the top sheet.

"May I ask you about this bag? It is, by far, the ugliest thing I've ever had the misfortune of seeing," he asked her.

"Yes, I know, but I need it." She looked at him and saw the blatant curiosity in his eyes. "No, I guess I needed it. It was your mother's idea, actually, to make this thing."

"Mom's? Oh no, she wouldn't have been caught dead with that color paisley. I know. When I was in first grade, I made her this bracelet thing out of those brightly colored beads they have. It was so pink, it defied reason. She told me it was very lovely, but pink, especially Barbie pink, was not her thing. I took it back to school the next day and made the art teacher let me make her one that was all black. Mom wore it for years."

Morgan smiled at the memory. "No, she didn't give it to me; she tricked me into making it. My hand had been...I had to crush my hand between the top of the bed Randall had me cuffed to and the concrete walls to escape from him. He'd gone up to the main part of his house to get his gun to kill me, he'd said.

"I'd been raped, you see. Not just by him, but several of his friends too. He'd kidnapped me and kept me tied in his basement as entertainment for him and his buddies. I didn't care...I didn't care if I died, but there was no way he was living. So I got away and killed him.

"Physical therapy hadn't been started soon enough, so I needed to have my hand broken again to have the bones set correctly. I refused to do the exercises.

"Your mom was one of the regular people who came in and gave those silly pep talks and whatever. She once told us how we could make a better life for ourselves. If we just applied as much energy into getting up off our collective asses and getting reformed as we did trying to hustle people, we'd be millionaires. She wasn't a popular speaker.

"She told me that if I made this bag and made it well enough that it didn't fall apart the first time I used it, she'd never pick at me again to do crafts with her. Anything would be worth not having to do crafts. She used enough glitter and glue on stuff it looked like Tinker Bell threw up on us.

"It took me nine months to cut the material out perfectly. I had to read up on how to use a pattern first, you see. Then it took me another six months to make my hand wrap around the scissor handles. It was only nine pieces of material, and I had to cut some of the pieces out four times before it was right. The sewing machine posed another problem. I had to gently guide the material through the foot and not screw up the thread too. I'd never worked on anything so hard in my life. And true to her word, I never did another craft with her. She also got me another trial. Once the DA looked my sheet over, they decided it was a miscarriage of justice and I got out." She looked down at her plate, just realizing that she hadn't spoken that much in five years.

"Poor Morgan. It can be bad enough to be stuck in a whole house with Mom, but at least I can step outside. Being stuck inside a prison without the ability to escape must have been like a nightmare." She laughed with him. She liked this Grant. He was fun and smart.

By the time lunch was over and he paid the bill, she was going to meet him at his studio a week from Friday.

CHAPTER
TWENTY-EIGHT

"This is a really nice camera. I'd like to buy it from you. That is, if you'll take payments. I don't have a lot of ready cash like this." She didn't have any cash at all and they both knew it.

Byron thought about it for a few minutes, listening to the shutter click and the flash light before answering. He knew that she'd hate the idea of owing him money, but she needed it. "Keep it."

"This is a really expensive camera. I can't keep it. I'll make you payments." She took six more pictures while he waited.

"How expensive? You know, I don't care. I don't want it, you do. So what's the problem?"

"The problem is that it's a really expensive, top of the line camera. It practically does all the work for me. And it costs almost six grand."

He watched her stiffen. He loved making her mad. She got all indignant and stuffy when she was. "Really. Wow, Toni must have wanted something really nice to have spent that much on me." He didn't like talking about Toni, but somehow, telling Morgan didn't feel so whiny. He put the finished piece of pottery on the shelf next to him and looked at Morgan. "It's from my ex-wife. Whenever she spent money on me, she wanted twice as much spent on her. Toward the end of our marriage, I stopped caring what she spent and she stopped being discreet about her affairs. It ended. That particular gift has been sitting in my spare bedroom since a couple of years before our divorce. So, as a favor to me, I'd like for you to have it. If you don't take it, Morgan, I'll make sure that it's in the next pick up for the trash company just to spite you." He watched as she glared at him.

"Thank you. I'll...I promise to think horrible thoughts of Toni every time I use it. And I'm sorry. I didn't mean to bring up..." She swayed suddenly and grabbed for something to catch herself. He jumped up from the chair he was sitting in and made a grab for her.

"Sit down. There's a chair just behind you." He gently lowered her into the chair and pushed her head between her legs as she slumped forward. She took several deep, calming breaths.

"I haven't been...I forgot to eat this morning, that's all. I'm okay now, you can let me up."

"No, you'll stay there just a little while longer while I get my heart out of my throat. Morgan, I swear if you try to sit up once more, I'm going to paddle you." When he thought he could walk without falling on his own face, he spoke to her again. "I'm going over to the fridge and get you a pop. You'll stay here until I get back, you hear me?"

"I'm not a child. And I don't want a pop. It has a lot of calories in it that I don't want." He growled and went and pulled the can from the little refrigerator anyway.

Unwanted calories. If she didn't need those extra calories, he'd eat his next commission check.

"Here, drink this, and shut up about it. I'm going to ask you some questions. You aren't going to like them, but I expect you to answer them." He took the can from her and popped the tab and handed it back to her. When she didn't drink right away, he lifted her hand and the cola to her mouth.

"What kind of questions? I'm fine, really." She didn't try to get up this time, but did continue to glare at him.

"You've been coming here for what now, five weeks? In that time, this is the fourth time you've gotten dizzy. When was your last menstrual cycle?" Her mouth opened and closed several times before she reached out and pushed him to his butt.

"None of your business. What are you, pretending to be a doctor? I haven't had sex since I was raped. Satisfied? That was five years ago. I'm reasonably sure if I was gonna get pregnant, I'd have figured it out by now. Even you should know that much about the birds and the bees."

"Are you saying you and Nicky didn't have sex at Thanksgiving? Because if you didn't then I..." When she paled to a deathly shade of white and looked at him, he knew in that moment every name he'd called Nicky that day was true. The lying bastard had taken advantage of her. "I'm going to kill that son of a bitch."

"No, I can't be...he didn't...he...I'm going to be sick." She stood so suddenly that he didn't have the chance to stop her, but let her go tearing to the bathroom in the back of the shop.

After a few minutes, he stood up and went to the door. Listening carefully, he heard the water running and her crying softly on the other side of the door. He knocked gently and waited for her to answer. Just when he was about to knock again, she answered him.

"I just need a few minutes." He didn't move, but waited for her to come out. "He told me that...he didn't finish, you see. He said that he wasn't going to let me trap him. I didn't know what he was talking about. He thought... he said that I was trying to trap him into marriage. Marriage. I wasn't. Your nephew was doing a book report on his hero and he'd asked me to help. I was doing research all right, but not how he thought. Jacob had thought of his Uncle Nick as a hero." He heard her sobbing again and his heart hurt for her.

Bryon now understood her terror at finding him in the restaurant that first day. She'd been afraid of Nicky showing up. And he remembered that report that Jacob had done on Nicky. Jacob had won first prize for it. They'd gone to lunch at the school together just last week.

Byron wanted to go into town and find his brother and castrate him. Slowly. And with relish. Fucking prick. He wondered what else had been said between them. It had to have been enough to drive her from the house in the middle of the night. She had opened her foot wound and had bled all over the staircase and pooled in the kitchen where she'd used the phone. There had been blood on the receiver when they'd come down that morning.

"Morgan, honey, are you all right?"

Byron realized that she'd been quiet for a little while and he was worried. He tried to take inventory of the room, wondering if there were any drugs or sharp knives or anything she could be using. He didn't think so, but if she didn't answer soon, he was going to break down the door. He stepped back when he heard the lock click and the door opened slowly. When she did finally come out, her eyes were swollen and red.

Byron wanted to hug her, hold her tightly in his arms, but he knew she wouldn't like that. He also knew that she wouldn't take his sympathy either.

"I think I have enough pictures for now. I... if I need anything else...I wanna go home, Byron, okay?"

Morgan's eyes welled up with tears again and he stepped closer and pulled her into his arms anyway. She was stiff at first, and then she sagged against him and cried again. He knew that he was saying things to her, but couldn't for the life of him make sense of it. He hurt for her.

CHAPTER TWENTY-NINE

Pregnant. If she was, and she wasn't admitting to anything right now, then she'd be ten weeks. She rubbed her hand over her flat belly and shuddered. A baby. Nickolas' baby. He would never believe her.

Morgan had made Byron promise that he wouldn't say anything to anyone. Not even his mother. Especially not his mother. It could be just a mistake.

"Right. A mistake. You are living in a fantasy world if that's what you think. I won't tell anyone, but you have to go and have a test done. Immediately. Take it to Damon. He can be discreet, and if he doesn't, then I'll kill him too."

"*No*! No killing. Promise me. I'll go take one of those home thingies and see if ...I'll take one tomorrow. Do you promise not to murder anyone? I've been to prison and you'd never make it on the inside. You're much too pretty. You'd be someone's boy-toy in no time flat."

"I promise. But you have to go to Damon if it turns out positive. If you don't, then I'm going to take it back."

"All right. Okay."

She'd gone into three different drug stores on the way home.

The buses she had to take to get home stopped that many times, and she made that many purchases. At the first one, she bought three tests and a calendar. She wanted to make sure of her dates. And sitting in the parking lot of the second store waiting for the next leg of her journey, she realized that she hadn't had a period since before Halloween. At the next stop, she bought four more tests, two candy bars, a can of chips, and a box of condoms. When she came out of the third shop, she had four more tests and three bags of stuff she didn't remember purchasing.

When she opened the door to her room, she emptied all the bags on the table and sat down and cried again. She had purchased a total of eleven tests, two bags of candied hearts that said things on them, stables for a stapler she didn't own, a toothbrush, hair spray that she never used, the can of chips, seven candy bars, three boxes of condoms and an infant sleeper. Bright blue.

Morgan didn't sleep a wink all night. She had laid all four of the tests out on the back of the toilet that night before going to bed, wanting to be ready in case she had to pee sometime in the middle of the night. Of course, she couldn't have peed if her life depended on it right now, but she wanted to be ready.

By eight-thirty, she got up and took the first test. She was shaking so badly that she wasn't even sure she'd hit the mark. She pulled open the second one before she'd even set the timer for the first one. She laid both sticks on the counter and left the room. If she sat there watching them, she'd go nuts...well, nuttier anyway.

When the timer went off, Morgan took a deep breath and looked at the little windows. Both were positive. She sat down hard on the toilet and stared at them. She must have done something wrong, she thought, and wondered vaguely if she could pee again.

Pregnant. Almost three months. What was she going to do now?

A knock on her door startled her sometime later. When she looked at her watch, she couldn't believe it was almost noon. She'd been in the bathroom for four hours. Nervously, she looked at all eleven boxes of pregnancy tests opened and strewn all over the room. She had peed on twenty-two sticks and all of them read the same. Positive. The knock again, harder and louder this time, had her leaving the bathroom and running to the door. She looked in the peep hole and there stood Byron.

"Not now. Go away, please. I'm...I just took a shower and I'm not dressed yet." Well, that was partly true, she had taken a shower, and she wasn't dressed yet.

"Morgan, open the damned door before I break it down. Damon is with me and he has a few things to go over..."

She ripped the door open so quickly that he jumped back. "Are you fucking nuts? What part of 'promise me you won't say anything' did you not understand? Go away. We have nothing to discuss. You stupid jackass, I can't... I suppose the whole family knows? Damn it." She stomped her foot and winced.

Byron paid her little mind and walked right in. Damon stood back for maybe ten seconds, and then he barged right in too. Both men sat down on the couch and looked at her.

"Sure, come on in. Make yourselves at home. Can I get you a drink, maybe something to eat?" If they couldn't hear the sarcasm in her voice, she'd worry about them.

"No, thanks, but when did you eat last? Byron, go in the kitchen and find her something to eat. I'm betting she forgot to eat. How many test have you taken? Byron, bring her some tea if she has some, if not, lots of juice. Morgan, sit down before you fall down."

Morgan sat, but not because he told her to, but because she was suddenly dizzy again. That one word kept running through her head. Pregnant. Pregnant. Pregnant. Over and over until she wanted to scream.

"Twenty-two. I used all of them. What am I gonna do? I don't have the means to raise a baby on my own. I barely have enough for myself." She looked around the room she rented over the bar. There wasn't even room for a crib much less a toddler.

"Let's cross that bridge in a minute. Right now, I want to take a blood test and confirm your twenty-two other tests, all right?" Damon was telling her gently.

Morgan barely registered Byron's comment on the tests she'd taken. Didn't even notice when Damon rolled up her robe and gently took out some of her blood. She just lay back on the chair and closed her eyes. Suddenly, she was so tired.

It was dark out when she woke up. There was a tantalizing smell coming from somewhere close and she realized how hungry she was. She sat up slowly and tried to remember getting into bed again, then remembered Byron and Damon and why they were there.

Morgan heard them then, or at least she supposed it was them. She didn't want to talk with them just yet and went into the bathroom. Someone had cleaned up and had taken out the entire mess along with the boxes and bags. She was grateful for that. She didn't think she could look at them again.

After a very long hot shower, she got dressed and went to the door. She had given herself a good talking to while in the shower and felt better equipped to deal with whatever happened now. Hell, maybe the tests she'd taken were faulty and she wasn't ... yeah right and she could live with the Easter Bunny and Santa Claus when she got hugely round.

"Hello. You hungry? I have linguine and marinara sauce. Garlic bread and a salad. You didn't have much in the way of food, so we went shopping while you were napping. Come on while it's hot." Damon had cooked for her. Whatever had happened with the tests, it wasn't good.

"Tell me." She didn't move as Byron came into the little kitchenette and sat down next to his brother.

"You're pregnant. As I'm sure you'd already figured out. If what we think happened when we think it did then I'd say you're due around the first of September, give or take five days."

"*If* you think happened *when* it happened? You mean when I had sex? Yes, well that's my business. I thank you for your concern, but I'd like you two to leave now. I have to ... I have things to do." She walked over to the door and opened it wide. Neither of them moved.

"Is it Nicky's baby, Morgan? Because if it is, then you're wrong if you think it's not our concern. Nicky will stand up for you and that child. I'll...we'll make sure he does," Damon said. She glanced over at Byron. He shook his head slightly. He hadn't told him.

"No, it's mine and only mine. I'd like for you both to leave now. I appreciate your concern, but it's nothing to do with you. Any of you. If you send me a bill, I'll pay you for your time." Damon stared at her. She didn't squirm or fidget like she normally did when people were disappointed in her, but stared right back.

"Come on, Damon, let's go. She's right. It's none of our concern," Byron said to his brother. Finally, Damon stood up, too, and walked toward the door. She wanted to cry with relief, but stood her ground.

"Here is a list of doctors in the Zanesville area that will take good care of you. This is a prescription for prenatal vitamins that you need to start taking right away. Stay off your feet as much as possible and eat lots of fruit. If you can't afford anything, and I mean anything, Morgan, you call me." She took the offered sheets from him, but didn't say a word. She was afraid that if she opened her mouth, she'd beg them to take care of her.

After she heard them pull out of the lot, she sat down at the table again. Without a thought as to what she was eating, she filled her plate and began putting the food into her mouth, chewed, swallowed, then did it again until the plate was empty. Getting up, she began cleaning up the kitchen and going over the layout of the pictures she'd taken yesterday—*was it only yesterday?*—of Byron's art. After she'd cleaned up, she pulled her laptop to her and began setting the pages up. She got up twice to use the bathroom and to get a drink of water. Not once did she think of the baby or Nickolas Grant.

CHAPTER THIRTY

"Do you think its Nicky's baby?" They'd been driving for about ten minutes when Damon asked him. Byron was actually surprised that he had waited so long. He wasn't any closer on how to answer him than when they'd gotten in the car.

"Morgan is my friend, Damon. I...she said things when we figured it out that I don't think...she probably regrets saying to me."

"Like what? Did he rape her? I'll kill the son of a bitch."

That had been Byron's first thought, too, when he'd figured it out, but he knew it wasn't true. He'd seen the way his brother had looked at her during dinner at Mom's. And the pain on his face at seeing her hurt at the apartment before they left for Thanksgiving. The apartment she'd been living in.

That apartment bothered him the most. Every time he thought about her living conditions while she'd lived there, he cringed. She had set up the bathroom like a small cell, her books all lined up on the long counter. Toothpaste and other toiletries were in a neat line on a hand towel that he knew he'd never owned. First, because it was neon bright pink. Secondly, it was bright pink. Morgan had only lived in the bathroom and used the kitchen as a sort of mess hall. The single fork, spoon, and knife were on the counter along with her white plate, bowl, and mug. There wasn't a glass in the whole room. There was a whole case of dried noodles sitting on the counter next to the stove in a variety of flavors and nothing in the fridge. The only thing in the freezer had been Nicky's credit card. When Mick had come by to get her things on the Saturday after Thanksgiving, the only thing he took was her cash and the sleeping bag, which had been laid out in the tub like a cot. He also grabbed her clothes, all of which had been neatly folded and put in a plastic grocery sack in the bottom of the linen closet. The money had been taped to the bottom of the sink drawer in a folded newspaper. She had two-hundred-thirty-three dollars.

Neither man had said a word about either the way she lived, nor why he was picking up her things.

Both men were quiet for about thirty minutes when Damon startled Byron out of his thoughts. "If it is his, which I'm betting it is, then do you think we should say something to him?"

"No. She'd kill us both. I think we should just do this her way. If we don't...I'm afraid she'll run. I don't want to lose her."

"Are you in love with her, Byron?" Byron had told Damon that he'd had Morgan doing a web design for his work and that he'd seen her a lot over the past few months. He never mentioned whose baby it was, or what he thought.

"Yes. No. Not the way you think. I love her, but like a baby sister. She's a great kid, so yeah, I guess I love her."

Damon didn't say anything for the rest of the ride to Columbus and the Grant building. "I really like her, too. Byron, did you notice she didn't ask about an abortion?" He shut the door to the car and was gone before he could form an answer. No, he hadn't noticed. But he was glad she hadn't.

~~~

"Are you gonna keep it?" Mrs. Sugar asked her. She wanted

to answer her unequivocally yes, but she wasn't stupid. She couldn't raise a baby on her own. She had no job, no insurance, and no one to help her. As much as she wanted to, it just wasn't feasible.

She had told Mick and his wife that she was pregnant last week. If they were going to kick her out of the apartment, she needed to start looking soon. She was already three months gone and would need somewhere safe to stay until the kid was born.

"I'm not sure I can raise a baby. I don't know the first thing about them. I'm sorta leaning toward adoption right now." She couldn't look at her. The Sugars had been so kind to her, so supportive.

"Well, you have a few months yet. If you need help or have any questions, I'm just around the corner. And I can be a great Lamaze coach. I've raise nine children, so I got a little knowledge under my belt." When Mrs. Sugar started to leave, Morgan panicked.

"Wait! I need to know how long you're gonna give me. I know you don't really owe me anything, but I would … "

"What are you going on about, child? Give you time for what?"

Morgan flushed all the way to her toes. "Aren't you gonna toss me out? I know that I'm pregnant and I have no right, but I need just a little time. I've just started working again, making some money. I don't have any insurance and the three doctors I called are really, really expensive. One guy wanted me to pay up front for the whole delivery. I don't have eleven thousand dollars just lying around. The vitamins were fifty-three dollars a month and that was with a coupon. I can be out by the end of the month, if that's okay with you?" Morgan wiped at the tears running down her cheeks. She'd like to blame it on hormones, but she knew it was because she felt like a failure to them. And to herself.

Mrs. Sugar sat down again and stared at her. "Are you...yes, I can see that you are. Morgan, love, why would I toss you out because you're pregnant? I love having you close. I plan to be this child's honorary grandmother. If you keep it, that is."

Morgan looked around the room. It was all she had in the world. She had bought the furniture from them last month. She knew they gave it to her at a great discount. She'd been to garage sales and had seen what things were going for. And next month, she was going to buy herself a new computer, maybe. She looked down at the small mound that was a baby. She was four months pregnant as of today.

"I can't possibly keep it. The father, he... I'd have no help. I don't want to even be pregnant. I...I don't know how to be. I don't know how to love it. Someone else will be able to. There are lots of people who would be happy for a baby."

Mrs. Sugar didn't say anything for some time. "Morgan? Have you told the father about the baby yet? He has a right to know, both legally and morally. Maybe he'll change his mind."

"He...when we...he only had sex with me to prove something, a point I didn't get. Not then anyway. He told me that I wasn't going to trap him into marriage with a child. He even offered to pay me to have future sex with him. So, no, I don't think he's gonna change his mind."

"Bastard. Some men want to play but not pay. I'm a retired lawyer, but I still practice now and again. I'll write up the form letter for you. You have to let him know regardless of his opinion of himself. I'll give him ten days to respond to it. If he doesn't, then you've fulfilled your obligation to him. I'll bring it by tomorrow. What's his name?"

His name. Did she want people to know his name? No, not really. She didn't care about him one whit, but she also didn't want to have to explain to people how she had ever considered herself in the same league as the Grants. She didn't think he'd respond, but she also didn't want him to sue her for some sort of slander either.

"Can I just mail it to him, or does his name need to be on it?" If she could just send it, she could avoid as much contact as possible.

"When I write this for you, I will never be able to tell anyone anything you tell me. Ever. I won't even tell Mick. He'd probably kill him anyway and I don't have time to visit him in prison. Besides, who would cook for the bar? I need his name, I'm sorry."

"I see. Doctor Grant. Nickolas Grant." She looked away from Mrs. Sugar. She didn't want to see what she thought of her being with a man like Nickolas Grant.

"I'll have it for you in a few days. And, Morgan? It takes two people to make a child, not one. He was just as much a part of your being pregnant as you were.

CHAPTER THIRTY-ONE

"Becky Morgan? Ms. Becky Morgan?" The nurse had to shout to be heard above the din.

"That's me, well, sort of. It's Morgan Becky; Morgan is my first name, not my last." The clinic was extremely busy today. She had been there since eight this morning and it was now going on two. Her back hurt and she had to pee really, really bad. The lady at the desk had told her if she missed when they called her name, she would have to start at the top again. So she wasn't chancing starting this day all over.

"It says right here that it's Becky Morgan. I don't see nothing that says Morgan Becky." The woman looked to be in her mid-twenties, Morgan thought. She was chewing gum and popping it like it was going to be the next Olympic sport and she was going for the gold.

"No, it says Becky comma Morgan. The form said to give last name first, the first name last. That's what I did. So it's Morgan Becky. Sorry."

"Really, that's a comma? Well, duh. Look, I don't care what your friggin' name is. You wanna go see the doctor or not, Miss Becky comma Morgan?" Miss Steele comma Linda was gonna get her nose punched if she didn't take it down a notch, thought Morgan.

"I want to see the doctor, please." She followed her back to a little room and was told to sit. When Morgan had asked if she could use the bathroom first, Linda didn't answer but left her sitting there.

Morgan had gone to see all the doctors on the list that Damon had given her. Two of them had refused to take her as a patient because she was uninsured. The third one had told her that she needed to pay up front. She couldn't do that, she told him. He had suggested that she take out a loan to pay the bill. And just what was she supposed to use as collateral, her belly?

The fourth doctor had a waiting list until mid-May. She'd be about seven months by then and she didn't think that would be very smart. The last doctor, a Dr. Simon, was nice enough, but he was really expensive and she didn't know how she could afford to see him and eat too. But she'd made an appointment for next month all the same.

When the door to the office opened and Dr, Clare stepped in, Morgan was almost relieved. Almost.

"Ms. Morgan. I understand you got smart with one of my staff. I don't want smart asses in my clinic. Your type of people think that just because it's free you can treat anyone how you want. That's not the way things are done here."

"I didn't get smart with anyone. I just corrected her when she said my name wrong. It's Morgan Becky, not Becky Morgan. And just what 'type' is my kind?"

"You will tone down that attitude right now, or I'll have your butt back in prison so fast your head will spin."

Morgan sat there for several seconds just looking at Dr. Clare. Prison. If it wasn't for the fact that having the baby in prison went against everything she knew, she'd let her. Instead, she leaned over and picked up her bag and left the office. She didn't need prenatal care that badly.

"Don't bother coming back here either!" was shouted down the hall after her. She didn't even look back, but raised her hand and flipped her off. Maybe it was childish, she thought, but it was the first smile she'd had since she'd found out she was going to have a baby.

~~~

"Dr. Grant? I'm a processor; I have a registered letter for you." Nick and Damon were just leaving Nick's apartment when the man showed up. Nick looked at his brother.

"Is there a first name? We're both Dr. Grant." Ever helpful Damon. He couldn't think of any reason why he'd be served, so it had to be for Damon.

"Ah, yeah... Hummm... I have to call the office. I can't read this here name. Hang on a second." As the man stepped away and pulled out his cell phone, Nick looked at his brother.

Something was up. He looked...nervous. *Oh no*, he thought, *Damon is in trouble.* Someone was suing him for malpractice or something. Shit. He was just pulling out his own cell when the man came back.

"Nickolas. It's for Nickolas Grant. That either of you two?" To say that Nick was shocked would have been an understatement. It wasn't until Damon nudged him that he realized that he hadn't answered him.

"Yes. Me, that's me, Are you sure it's for Nickolas, not Damon? I can't think why the law firm of...Sugar and Sugar would be contacting me?" *Why did that name sound familiar?* he wondered.

"Thanks, asshole. Just tip the man and let's go get some dinner. I'm starving and you owe me ribs." Damon poked him in the ribs as he walked away.

Nick signed the receipt for the letter and moved to the elevator where Damon was waiting. He stuck the letter in his jacket pocket and stepped on when the doors opened. *Sugar. Who was Sugar?* he thought.

"Are you going to open it? Might be important."

He looked over at his brother again. He knew. He didn't know how he knew, but Damon knew what the letter was about.

"Why don't you tell me what it says and I won't have to bother?"

"How the hell should I know what it says? Just open the fucking thing and let's forget about it."

Ah, Damon was not only nervous, but he was snarky as well. He pulled out the letter and handed it to him. "Read it. Tell me what it says then." This was a joke one or all of them were pulling on him. His birthday was tomorrow, and they thought they'd have fun at his expense. He watched Damon's face as he debated with himself and finally tore it open. "Damon?" He had fallen back against wall when he opened the letter and, just like that, Nick knew that it wasn't a joke.

"It says...it's to inform you that Morgan Becky is pregnant. She's contacting you of her pregnancy and telling you that you have no legal rights to her or her child and that she isn't asking for your support or name. As one of the men she has had sex with in the past year, she is legally notifying you of her impending delivery."

"What?" He took the letter from Damon and read it himself. There had to be a mistake. Morgan was pregnant? It wasn't possible. "It's not mine. I didn't ejaculate inside her. This is just a ploy to get money from me. Well she isn't..."

Nick opened his eyes and looked up at David Tulle. He blinked several times before the man came into focus.

"What happened? I don't remember...I was talking in the elevator and I don't remember what happened next."

"I hit you, you fucking asshole. Didn't ejaculate? Are you fucking nuts? What, you relied on the pull and pray method much? If you do, then its small wonder I don't have fifty bastard nieces and nephews running around."

Damon had hit him? Because Morgan was pregnant? Was he named in the letter too? No that couldn't be right... Still.

"Could you be the father too?" When Damon advanced on him with fury in his eyes, David pulled him back. Nick knew he wasn't the baby father any more than he was. He'd get to the bottom of this right now. He pulled out his cell phone to call Devin. "Yeah, I need your help. I've been named in a paternity suit and I want my name out of the hat for daddy of the year."

"Like that's fucking a possibility," Damon snarled at him. Devin must have heard him and laughed at Nick.

"So, who's the babe in question? Let me guess...Bambi Jenkins? No! Wait, that vamp from Damon's office, what's her name?" Devin asked him.

"It's Morgan Becky."

"Nah, that's not it. Morgan is the woman who used to work for... Holy shit! You knocked up Morgan? Mom is gonna castrate you. Twice. Shit, really? Morgan? I thought she had better taste than that."

"Funny. Yes, it's Morgan Becky. I was just served by Sugar and... Shit." He just remembered where the name came from. Mick Sugar, the bar owner.

"Sugar and Shit? I don't think I've ever heard of them. And, believe me, I'd remember a law firm by that name."

Nick thought, for not the first time, that his entire family was a bunch of sarcastic pricks.

"Can you help, or do I need to find a more reputable firm to help me? I'm not the father. I want her to stop insisting that I am. What can you do?" Nick rubbed his chest again. Damn it, he'd not had an ulcer flare up in two weeks. Of course, he wasn't eating well, but that didn't matter really.

"You say you're not the father, then forget about it. Fax me the paperwork and I'll see what I can do. We may have to order a paternity test, just to be safe, but that's no biggy. Wow, Morgan Becky. Didn't see that one coming."

He stayed on the phone with him until Devin received the fax. He wanted to get this cleared up as soon as possible.

"It's a form letter telling you that she's pregnant. I'm going to demand proof of that now. I'm having Caroline call the doctor. It says here that you are named as one of the men that had sex with her in the past year. I'm assuming this isn't true?"

He'd had sex with her, but he hadn't come. He was really stupid for not thinking he could still get her pregnant at the time, but he'd been so furious at her. "Yeah, I had sex with her. Once, and it wasn't all that great either." That was a lie. It had been absolutely heaven being inside of her. But he was not sharing that with his brother, any of them. And he wasn't going to tell them how much he missed her, how much he wanted to find her and to tell her he was an ass. Well, up until today that is.

"Well, that puts a different slant on things. Let me order the DNA test and we'll work from there. I'll be at Mom's on Sunday for Mother's day. I'll see you then."

CHAPTER THIRTY-TWO

"I'd like to suggest you first find another doctor. You look like shit. You're supposed to glow when you're pregnant; you just look sickly. Secondly, give him what he wants."

Morgan looked at Mrs. Sugar. She knew how bad she looked, but the doctor said the baby was fine. He also told her he didn't want a fat woman delivering. So he'd put her on a three thousand calorie a day plan. Morgan wanted her baby to be healthy when it was born. No one wanted to adopt a sickly child. She'd learned that all those years in the orphanage.

The diet was working out okay. She was saving money on her food bill, which was good. And she only had four months and four payments of a thousand dollars a month to have him paid off. Money was tight.

"I don't care. Just set it up. It doesn't matter." She rubbed her hand down her belly and felt the kid move under her hand.

The first time it had moved, she wept for an hour. There was a life inside of her. It moved around a lot at night, keeping her awake. But she didn't rub it anymore, not unless she forgot, like now. It was hard not to touch it. She couldn't fall for it. It needed a home with loving parents and someone who could watch over it. It wasn't going to be her.

"Just set it up and let me know." She waddled back upstairs

to her rooms above the bar and sat on the kitchen chair. She reached into her pocket and pulled out the blue sleeper she'd bought that first day. As she laid it out on the table, she began to cry softly. When it was neatly spread out, Morgan laid her head down on it and began to cry harder.

~~~

"She's agreed to the test. It'll be performed on Monday the second of June. There were a couple of conditions that I didn't think you'd have a problem with, so I agreed to them. Her attorney and I will be there as witnesses and Damon has agreed to do the tests," Devin told him as soon as they shut the study room door at their mom's. He'd not told her yet, and didn't plan on it either.

"What conditions?" He had wanted to be there when the test was performed, but Damon still wasn't talking to him and he was still pissed at him too. He'd just wanted to see the look on her face when she had to come face to face with him after all her lies. Devin said that would be in bad form and to just stay at home.

"That after the tests, you will give up all rights to the child. I think she's giving it up anyway, so that shouldn't be too hard. Also, that you'll pay for the tests. I didn't think you'd have a problem with that either. Was I right?"

Morgan wasn't keeping her baby? That didn't make any sense. Hadn't she gotten this way to have something to hang around his neck for all time? He didn't know what to think about that.

"Yeah. Fine, whatever." He was still frowning as he followed Devin out of the office. How was she paying for any of this? Were the adoptive parents paying for the bills? Maybe that was her angle.

The phone was ringing when he came into the kitchen. His Aunt Pea asked him to answer it for her; she was expecting a call from her friend about some auction or something.

"Grant. Hummm...Parker residence." He almost hung up when there wasn't anything at the other end for several seconds.

"Dr. Grant? It's Shannon Fist from the hospital. You need to come here now. I think that fool is trying to kill her," Shannon was whispering urgently.

"I think you have the wrong Dr. Grant. Let me get my brother." He started to put the phone down, but her yelling suddenly had him putting it back to his ear.

"No, you have to tell him to get here now. She's in bad shape and he... Yes, Dr. Simon, I was just giving the results from the hemoglobin tests to Dr. Grant. He needed them stat. Yes, I'll make sure that Ms. Becky is released as soon as billing talks to her."

Nick's heart skipped several beats when she mentioned Morgan's name. She was hurt, in bad shape. Christ, what had she done now? He realized he was holding a dead phone when the beeping started.

"*Damon!* We have to go now. Morgan's hurt and some guy named Simon is going to kill her." He knew he wasn't making any sense, but Damon was following and that was all that mattered. He was getting into his SUV when he noticed his entire family was rushing out the door after him. *Shit!*

"Mom, you don't need to come. I'm sure that..."

"You will not finish that sentence, or so help me, Nickolas Patrick Grant, I will paddle your butt but good. Get in this monstrosity and let's get moving." She simply opened the front door and crawled in.

"You are such a dead man when she finds out about Morgan. You'd better hope the kid is yours, because it will be all that's left of your lineage when Mom skins you alive." He watched Damon get into the car next to Devin and Jamie. Spencer, Dan and Meggie were in their own car. Shit, he was so dead.

The hospital was busy, extremely busy. As soon as they pulled in, Damon jumped out of the car and flew through the ER doors. Everyone else followed. Nick was just parking his vehicle when security stopped him.

"You can't leave that car there. It's for doctors and emergencies. You can park over in the visitor's lot over to the South," Officer Carlton told him.

"My brother is a doctor here, Damon Grant. He's just inside. I brought him in for an emergency."

"That's right nice of you, but you still ain't parking there. There's a visitors lot over on the South side of the building. You just hop back on in that thing and park it over there." He started to argue that he was one of the Grants who paid for the entire neonatal clinic, the Grant Neonatal Clinic, but didn't think it would be worth the effort. He'd still end up on the South side of the building in the visitor's parking lot. It was a good twenty minutes later before he walked into the ER.

"They won't let us see her yet. Damon is upstairs with the head of medicine arguing about her care. Did the nice person tell you what happened? They won't tell me anything." He pulled his mother to him. If by the end of the day, she killed him, he wanted to have this one warm memory to take to his grave with him.

"Mom, there's something I need to tell you. It's about Morgan. You're not going to like it, but Morgan is..." They all turned as one toward Damon as he came striding toward them talking.

"She's now in my care. I'm having her transferred to the second floor right now. As soon as I see her, I'll be right out to tell you what I can." And he disappeared through the doors again, this time to emergency.

No sooner had they started to sit down when they were up again. Even from where they were sitting, they could hear Morgan scream. Nickolas was through the doors and moving toward her before anyone thought to stop him.

Someone was holding one of her arms above her head and someone else was trying to — it looked to Nick — put a needle in her arm. She looked at him and screamed again.

"Get away from her! You're terrifying her, damn it." He moved the needle guy out of the way and moved beside Morgan. "I've got you, no one is gonna hurt you. Let her arm go. She can't stand to be touched like this. Morgan? Look at me, honey. No, not at him. Look at me."

When she turned to look at him, he saw with horror that someone had beaten her up. Her lip was swollen and bloody. It looked like her cheek was cut open to the bone and her right eye was swollen completely shut.

"Oh, baby, who did this to you?" He gently touched her jaw and when she whimpered, he wanted to hit someone.

"I wanna go home. Make them let me go, Nickolas. I wanna go home now." He wanted to give her anything she wanted, but knew that her injuries were worse than they looked.

"Let Damon look at you first. Then we'll see. Oh, honey, who did this?" He was going to find the person responsible and beat them to a bloody pulp.

"Nicky, I need you to step out, please. I need to examine her," Damon told him gently. Nick didn't want to leave her, but knew that he couldn't stay and watch either. Looking at her injured face was bad enough.

Nick nodded at his brother and walked around the curtain.

He could hear Damon talking to her, not what he was saying, but talking gently to her. He walked out into the waiting room to talk to his mom.

"Why didn't you tell me she was carrying your child?" Okay, maybe he didn't want to talk to his mom just now.

"I don't believe it's mine, that's why. We're having a paternity test done next month to determine who the father is." He just realized that he hadn't even noticed she was pregnant. Maybe the whole thing was a lie. She had also lost weight. He knew for a fact that pregnant women grew to as big as houses when they were expecting.

"So, there must be a possibility if you're having a test done. Am I correct in that at least?" He looked down at her. He was suddenly ten years old again.

"Yes, ma'am. Thanksgiving." He blushed. Christ, he'd just told his mother he'd had unprotected sex at her house on Thanksgiving.

"I see. This is May. Mother's Day, as a matter of fact. In the past, let me see, five months, you didn't think to mention that maybe you'd fucked a girl in my house, and knocked her up? Maybe at least mentioned it in passing how you got a girl, whom I've missed dearly, pregnant."

"It's not mine. So, no, I didn't think to mention it, in passing or otherwise." He looked over at Devin.

She turned on him like a hawk. "Did you know about this?" Devin looked panicky. He'd never been a good liar, which was why he becoming a lawyer had surprised everyone so much.

"Yes, ma'am. I'm representing Nicky in the case of wrongful slander against her." That sounded much worse than it was, he thought.

"I see. Who else knew about this? Damon, I presume. Who

else? Which of your other brothers were in on this?" It was the look. She was penetrating his brain, he just knew it.

"Byron. He was the first one to figure it out. He told Damon. I didn't find out until I was served with papers. She informed me and whoever else she'd slept with over the past year that she was pregnant."

"So the only two sons who didn't know about this were the two away at school. I see. No, I don't, but I will." She started to walk away, over to one of the really ugly green chairs, when she detoured around them and out the doors. He started to follow, but Dan's hand on his arm stopped him.

"I'd let her go if I was you. She's really mad, and if you follow her, she'll say things she'll regret."

He nodded. Nick had never disappointed his mother before. He ached like he never had about anything before in his life.

CHAPTER
THIRTY-THREE

Morgan was put into a private room on the maternity floor two hours later. She had protested long and hard, but, of course, no one listened. She pulled the blue sleeper up to her uninjured cheek and rubbed it there for several seconds, gathering her tears on the little garment.

The room was beautiful really. The TV was state of the art and huge. She didn't own a TV set herself. Had never found a reason to purchase one, not that she could afford one anyway. There was an overstuffed chair next to a fold out couch. The pretty little aide had told her it was there for anyone to spend the night if Morgan wanted them to. She was sure it would never be used. The floors were a very nice wood and the bank of cabinets behind her bed held all the equipment to use in case there was an emergency, she'd been told. The bed was a standard hospital bed, narrow and uncomfortable. She wasn't sure anything would be comfortable at this point, so didn't say anything when asked about it.

Nickolas had been in to see her twice since she'd been moved to this room. She hadn't spoken to him either time. He'd tried hard to get her to answer him, but she didn't have the energy, so she just closed her eyes and ignored him the best she could.

"Morgan? Would you talk to me please?" She closed her eyes. She didn't want to talk to Ms. Parker right now either.

She rolled over on her back, only moaning once, and pulled her hand with the sleeper in it under the sheet again. "Ms. Parker, I don't want to talk to anyone. I just want them to let me go home, but, of course, they won't. As for why I'm here, I'm not pressing charges and I refuse to talk about it." The police had been in to see her in the emergency room. She had told them that she didn't remember what had happened and that she was fine.

"All right, we won't talk about who hit you. For now anyway. I want to talk to you about the baby. Is it Nicky's?"

Morgan rolled back over to her side and pulled the sleeper to her cheek again. She didn't understand why the silly thing gave her comfort, but she'd been using it as a way to soothe herself for so long that she didn't try and figure it out anymore. She had just about broken herself of touching her belly about three weeks ago. But more and more, that had become harder to do too.

"It's no one's. I'm...it'll go to a good family as soon as it delivers. I'm not asking anything of anyone."

"It? You mean your child? Oh, Morgan, it's a child, not an 'it.' Turn around and look at me."

"No. I'm not becoming attached to something I can't have. Ms. Parker, I know you mean well, but this isn't any of your business. I did what was required of me by law. I notified all men who'd had sex with me recently and told them of my...my predicament. It in no way implied responsibility to anyone."

"I see. And just how many other men, other than Nicky, did you need to inform? Two, ten, two dozen? How many, Morgan?" she snarled at her.

Morgan didn't answer, but continued to stare blankly at the

couch no one would use. Why should she believe her when no one else did, she wondered? She knew that Nickolas didn't. If he had, then she wouldn't be having a DNA test done in an hour.

"Morgan, I'm..."

"I'm really tired, Ms. Parker. I'd like to take a nap, please. I think I'm going home tomorrow, so I'll tell you good-bye now." It was a long moment before she heard her moving around. When Ms. Parker touched her back briefly, she almost rolled over and asked for...she didn't know, but something. When the door clicked shut a few seconds later, Morgan gave into the tears and sobbed as quietly as she could into her pillow.

~~~

Nick sat in the chair in Damon's hospital office while Damon talked to someone on the phone.

Morgan was scheduled to have the test done in twenty minutes. And then they were going to perform an ultrasound. She'd never had one. Damon said that she should have had at least two by this far along in her pregnancy. He'd never heard why she hadn't. And for that matter, he'd never found out why Damon was now her acting doctor.

"That was Devin. He's across town, stuck in traffic. He can't make it to the test. He doesn't want to reschedule, so he suggested that you sit in as a witness. I don't know what Morgan will say, if anything."

"What's involved?" He didn't want to be witness to a blood bath. He hated the sight of blood, and women's tears were worse. He was sure with Morgan it would be ten times worst. Every time she hurt, it felt like a blow to his heart, he realized.

"What we're doing is an Amniocentesis test. I'll use the ultrasound to guide a thin needle into her uterus and through her abdomen. The needle will draw out a small amount of her amniotic fluid, and that's what we'll test."

"And the risks, what are they?" He knew from Devin that it was a pretty common thing to demand, even for married couples. People didn't trust much anymore.

"There's a chance that I could accidentally nick the baby. There's also a chance of her miscarrying. Morgan could also experience some cramping and a little leaking of amniotic fluid, maybe some vaginal bleeding."

"Miscarry? Does she know this? And she's okay with this?" He was shocked about that.

"I asked her; she didn't answer. But she did sign all the required paperwork when I asked her to."

Nick figured he was the only one she wasn't speaking to. He smiled at that. "Yeah, okay, I'll witness it. That's only if she answers you to the affirmative."

Fifteen minutes later, he was standing next to her bed in a tiny room with some expensive equipment. There were two women in the room besides Morgan. One of them was Mrs. Libby Sugar. The other was a nurse to assist Damon in the test.

Morgan wasn't looking at anyone. She had her back to the room when he walked in and hadn't turned around when Mrs. Sugar introduced everyone.

"Morgan, I need you to lie on your back, please, and try to lay still. I'm going to find the position of the baby then I'm..."

"Dr. Grant? Just do the test. Ms. Becky doesn't want any information. We've discussed this. Please, just finish up so that we can all move on," Libby said.

Nick looked down at Morgan. She had her left arm over her eyes and her body was trembling. He could see the tears streaming down the side of her face. He looked at Mrs. Sugar as she shook her head at him. Something wasn't right. He wasn't sure what it could be, but he knew it deep in his heart.

Nick looked over at Damon as he ran a flat instrument over Morgan's belly. When she jumped, he soothed her and asked her to lay still. Suddenly, the room was filled with the sound of a heartbeat. Loud and clear. Fast, the beating was so fast. Damon was looking at a little monitor and so he looked too.

Christ. There was a body, small and round. He could make out the beating then; the little heart was pulsing over and over. Then a hand pressed against the monitor, a tiny little hand with fingers so small that he could have put the whole thing into his watch pocket. He burst out laughing. A baby. Morgan had a baby in there.

Nick looked over to Damon just as he was pulling out a large friggin' needle. He felt himself sway slightly. He watched, mesmerized, as he slowly pushed the needle into Morgan's belly. Then he heard her whimper.

Blindly, he reached for her hand and when he touched the back of it, she grabbed him tightly. She clenched him once more, then pulled her hand away and pushed it under her back away from him. The tears were coming down faster now and she was shaking harder. He wanted to knock his brother away and pull her into his arms and comfort her.

"Almost done now, Morgan," Damon said to her. "You're doing great." He watched as he pulled the syringe out and put the tip into a vial and pushed the plunger into it. Clear liquid sprayed into it, and then he turned to Mrs. Sugar. "Mrs. Sugar, you need to take this and put it into the envelope and then seal it. Nicky, you need to initial that it is the fluid that I removed from Morgan Becky at sixteen-twenty."

Nick watched as the vial was verified, and he signed his name across the seal and then again on the receipt that he had watched the procedure. A courier was standing by to take the envelope to the lab on Seventeenth Street. When he went back to the little room, Morgan was gone. The nurse said that they took her to x-ray to do the ultrasound. She would be in her room in about an hour.

"Can I go with her? I'd like to...I don't know, I want to be with her, I guess." He didn't know why, but it seemed like he should.

"I'm sorry, Dr. Grant, but you aren't her family. Dr. Sheller is very strict about that. You could go back to her room and wait for her." He didn't know where she was, so he went back to her room to wait.

When they wheeled her in forty minutes later, he jumped up to help them lift her over to her freshly made bed. He'd been dozing off and on since he'd figured out the chair was as comfortable as it looked.

Morgan was pale and had been crying again. He could see how swollen her eyes were. He could tell she was fighting hard not to say something when the two guys dropped rather than laid her onto her bed. The nurse that came in with them ripped into the men in a heartbeat.

"Be careful, you lummox, she's hurting. Didn't anyone ever explain to you two that this is a hospital and people are hurt when they come in? We aren't supposed to hurt them more trying to care for them. Now, get out before I box your ears. Ms. Becky, Dr. Grant said that you could have something for pain if you'd like it. I think you should take it. You have a really nasty bruise," Nurse Fist told her.

"No. Thank you, but no. I'm okay."

Nick watched her roll to her side again. He thought she was trying to tune him out, but he wasn't having any of it, not today. He needed to talk to her and he needed her to stop crying. Rubbing his chest again, but more over his heart this time, he thought about crawling into the bed with her and holding her tight.

Ms. Fist glanced over his way, but didn't say anything. When she was out the door, he tried talking to Morgan again.

"Morgan, don't be an ass. If you hurt, take something for it." He knew that he could have worded that differently, but he didn't want her to hurt.

"Get out. I've taken your tests, now get out." She had said it so low, he wasn't sure if he'd heard her correctly.

"Morgan, honey, we need to talk about things. I think there has been a few things said that shouldn't have—"

"I'm not your honey and I said to get out. Now. Dr. Sheller said you'll have your results tomorrow. I want you to go away."

"Morgan, I want to..." He jumped back when she sat up quickly. Her lip was still swollen and her eye was still closed from the beating she'd taken yesterday. There looked to be about a dozen stitches in her cheek, sealing the deep wound. He didn't notice that, not right now. All he could focus on was her belly. In the move from the gurney to the bed, her gown must have shifted, exposing her entire swollen frame when she sat up.

Morgan's skin was tight and hard-looking along her abdomen. Her small frame looked oddly disproportional to the size of her belly. Her breasts had been full before. He remembered their weight and fullness in his hand and mouth. Now, they were larger and fuller than he remembered. Her nipples, a rosy shade of pink, were distended and darker. A deeper pink, almost rose. And then there were the bruises.

All along her ribs and arms were deep, purpling marks, some as large as his fist. There was a perfect imprint of fingers

where someone had wrapped their hand around her upper arm
and squeezed her hard. Her tight left thigh was bruised as well
with an angry cut that looked deep and painful. There was a
large bruise below her distended belly, just above her hip where
Damon had taken the sample from her.

"Ah, Morgan, honey. I'm so..."

"*Get out!* Get out now. Please, I beg you, just go away. Please,
just go away." She pulled the sheet over her and lay back down.
She was sobbing now, loud and hard. His heart broke for her. He
started to go to her, to make her let him hold her. But the nurses,
the entire shift, it looked to him, came rushing in at that moment.
One of them ushered him out and closed the curtain to surround
her bed. Even just on the other side of the door, he could still hear
her crying. He wasn't sure he'd ever forget the sound.

CHAPTER THIRTY-FOUR

"Come on, honey. You'll be all right. That man say something to you? I'll have one of them orderlies run him right outta the hospital. Bastard. Men, who the hell needs'em? Come on now, you're gonna throw up if you don't calm down."

Morgan just wanted everyone to go away. She body ached in ways and places she'd never realized, and her heart hurt in way she didn't realize it could. Damon had told her he'd be in to talk to her later tonight. Give her her options. Options. She didn't have a clue what sort of options he thought she might have, but she nodded to him anyway.

Nickolas still didn't believe her. Not that she really thought he would. Why should he? She'd tried to trap him, hadn't she?

When Damon had told her that Nicky was going to be a witness to the procedure, she wanted to shout at him, "No!" but Nickolas needed this for some sort of closure, and she wanted... she wanted to thumb her nose at him. He'd hurt her.

Morgan realized two weeks ago that she was letting him hurt her, and she resolved to do something about it. It was then that she realized that she loved him, despite all that had happened. Her foolish heart had decided that he was what it wanted and that was all there was to it.

When she pulled her hand to her cheek for the comfort, she

realized she didn't have her sleeper. She felt around under the sheet looking for it and couldn't feel the soft terry cloth anywhere. She'd had it last in the examining room down in x-ray. She needed her sleeper.

"I had a blue thing, a sleeper. Can you help me find it? I had it downstairs." The other nurses had left, but Shannon has stayed.

Morgan liked her. She was the kindest person she'd met in the hospital. Not that everyone else hadn't been great to her, but Shannon had been friendly and nice to her.

"I'll call down and see if you left it on the bed. You'll need to get another one of those, won't you?" Shannon walked out of the room and left Morgan wondering what she meant.

~~~

"Nicky, it's Byron. I'd like to know if you can meet me for dinner. I have something I'd like to discuss with you. It's important."

Nick didn't want to meet him or anyone. He wanted to go back to the hospital and sit with Morgan. But the staff had said she was having a really bad night and they'd had to give her something to relax. She was sleeping. He had actually thought he'd have a better chance of talking to her relaxed and half comatose, but he didn't think they'd agree.

"Yeah, okay. But a bar. I want a drink with dinner. Oh, and Damon is with me, is that okay?" Damon had been with him most of the early evening. Damon still wasn't speaking to him, but he'd been tagging along all the same.

"Yeah, sure. The more the merrier. Have you seen Morgan? I mean tonight. Have you been in to see her tonight?"

"No, I went by her room and the nurse said she was sleeping. Said she'd had a bad afternoon and had to sedate her." Nick had wondered about that too. Was it because it was less than twenty-four hours until truth time, or was there something else? She looked like she could use a good meal and several days of uninterrupted sleep.

"All right, I'll see you at that place on Tenth?"

Byron had just ringed off when his cell rang again. It was Spencer. "Hey, Spence. What's going on?" It was really late for him to be calling, at nine-thirty. He and Meggie were usually sound asleep.

"Meggie and I are in town for the night. We came in to see Morgan, but she's asleep. Meggie wants to know if you'll take her to dinner. She said you owe her." Nick smiled. Sure, Meggie wanted to have dinner with him.

"I was just going over to Bergen's with Damon and Byron. If she doesn't mind her other uncles coming along, I'll pay up there." He waited for him to relay the message to her and could hear her clapping her hands. It sounded like she was happy with the idea.

"Yeah, we'll meet you there. I wanna talk to you about something too."

This time, he made it all the way in the car before his phone went off again. His Mom. As Damon was driving, Nick put the phone to his ear to put on his seatbelt as he answered. "Hi, Mom. Everything okay?" Again, another early riser up past ten o'clock. He wondered if Dan was with her.

"Hello, Nicky. I was wondering if you'd like to have dinner with me tonight? I don't want to eat by myself. Also, I want to talk to you about something. It's really important." Her and everyone else, it seemed.

"Yeah, we're all going to go to Bergen's. You want to meet us there?" He was sure that nothing any of them had to talk to him about was going to bode well for him.

"Us? Who's with you now? Oh, my, here's Jamie and Devin. We'll all meet you there. If you hear from Dan, tell him to come there." And she hung up.

Great, he thought. All the gang was here now. Now he wished he'd driven his own car. Then if they made him too mad, he could just leave. Riding with Damon made for a less than graceful exit.

By ten-thirty, they were all seated in a huge private dining area. In addition to his brothers and Meggie were his mom, Dan, Jacob and James. It was almost eleven-thirty by the time they ordered and had their salads.

"This is very nice. I'm very glad you all are here in town tonight. Did anyone get to see Morgan earlier tonight?" His mother beamed around the table.

"Yeah, about that. How many of you are planning to be there tomorrow when the results come in?" Devin asked the room after the waitress left. Everyone in the room, including the children, raised their hands.

"Okay, let me rephrase that. How many adults are going to be there tomorrow? My office isn't big enough to house a brigade."

"Deal with it, young man. We all want to be there for Nicky. When will Morgan get the results, before or after?" His mother asked. "I'm assuming she won't be traveling to your office."

Nick hadn't thought of that. She was on bed rest until Tuesday morning. Then, he'd meant to ask Damon about her results of the examination, but had gotten side tracked by all the phone calls.

Nick saw Devin glance quickly at Damon. "What is it? What's going on with Morgan?" Nick asked sharply. He knew it was a little too sharp when Jacob backed up in his chair.

"She won't be getting the results. Mrs. Sugar is going to be there to answer any questions, but Morgan is... Morgan doesn't get the results. She doesn't want them," Devin said.

"What do you mean, she doesn't want them? How will she know..?" *Because she already knows*, he thought. She'd known all along who the father of her baby was. This had all been a... trick of some sort, a slick, sick trick. "Christ." Nick stood up. He suddenly needed to talk to her. He didn't have any clue what he was going to say, but he wanted to talk to her. He wished he'd never met her. No, that wasn't true. He wished he'd of done things differently, but he was very glad he'd met her. Very glad.

"Nick, I'm going to ask Morgan to marry me. Tomorrow, before the results are read," Byron said. He pulled a jeweler's box from his jacket pocket and set it on the table in front of his salad plate.

Nick was suddenly weak in the knees. It was a good thing he'd not stepped away from the table, he thought, or he'd be on his ass on the floor.

"Really? Not if I ask her first," Spencer said as he, too, pulled a blue box out of his pocket. Tiffany's. *Shit and double shit.* "I talked it over with Meggie, and she said she really liked Morgan. I think we could get along well enough." He pulled his daughter up in his lap as he spoke and smiled at her.

Damon didn't say a word, but put his baby blue box on the table, as well. Three brothers, three rings.

Damn it. They were not going to marry her. It wasn't their baby, and he had to do something to stop them from making the biggest mistake of their lives. He stood again and was just ready to blast them all to hell and back when Devin's phone shrilled in the silence.

"Grant."

Nick watched as he pulled out an electronic planner and started making notes with a stylist. Every once in a while, he would say something Nick couldn't understand and make more notes. "Yeah, he's here. Yeah, I'll bring him with me."

Morgan. Something to do with Morgan. He would bet his last commission check on it.

"I'm sorry, I have to leave. Hummm, Damon, I need you to come too. There's a problem and you're needed as well. Shannon said to tell you to turn your flippin' phone on."

"Shit. I forgot. What is it?" He pulled out his phone and because Nick was sitting next to him, could see that he had twenty-three missed calls.

"Morgan's just confessed to the murder of Alex Denty. They want to transfer her downtown for questioning. Libby Sugar can't represent her because of a prior commit with Denty's family. So she's asked me to step in. I'll meet you all back in my office first thing in the morning." As one, his family stood up and began pulling on jackets and picking up stray items off the table. Jacob began pulling on Meggie's sweater and picking up her crayons.

"I'm going with you," Nick told his brother.

"Well, of course she didn't," Margaret told the room in general. "She's just confused. We're all going to support her. Come along, we have to hurry. No telling what that child will tell them next."

He had to grin at his mother. She'd said just what he was thinking.

CHAPTER THIRTY-FIVE

Morgan was trying to keep her breathing under control, but wasn't having much luck. She'd do okay for a few minutes then look down at the handcuffs on her wrist that were attached to the bed rail and she'd panic. *Okay*, she thought, *I can do this*. But in reality, she knew she couldn't.

"Look at me. Breathe in and out and look at me." Nick's voice, so unexpected, had her turning toward him.

"What are you doing here? Go away. And I know how to breathe, you moronic jackass." When she started to look down at the cuffs again, he put his finger under her chin so that she could see only him.

"Morgan, have you always been this stubborn, or is it just me? I swear, I've never met a woman more frustrating in my life."

"It's you. And you are the king of frustration. Now, get out. You don't want to sully yourself with me, remember? You know, for someone who doesn't want anything to do with me, you sure insinuate yourself into my business a lot. *Get out!*"

"Shut up and breathe before you pass out. What do you think you're doing confessing to a murder without your lawyer present? Do you want to end up back in prison, for a lot longer this time?"

She jerked her chin away from him and looked across the

room. That's exactly what she was trying to do, actually. "You got your test, Dr. Grant, so now I would appreciate you leaving me alone. I don't want nor do—"

"Did you know that my brothers are planning to propose to you tomorrow? Yeah, Damon, Byron, and Spence. Meggie apparently approves of her daddy marrying you," he said with a smirk on his face.

Marriage? He had to be lying to her. Why would any of them want to...ah, the baby. They thought they'd ask her before the results were in so that when they found out it was a Grant, it could be kept in the family. For some reason, that hurt more than any of the physical pain she endured the past couple of days.

"I want you to leave me alone. I have a really nice family willing to take it as soon as it's delivered. I don't want anything from any of you. Especially you. Now, I'm not asking you again to get out."

The door opened then, and Devin Grant walked in, also the detectives from earlier tonight.

"Hello, Ms. Becky. Sir, we need for you to step out, please. We need to ask Ms. Becky some questions. You can wait in the hall." Detective Carol nodded to the door.

"No, I don't think so. I'm staying right here with her. And I'd like for you to take those cuffs off her. She is extremely upset with them there, and in her condition, I don't think she needs any extra stress right now." Nick crossed his arms over his chest and raised his eyebrow to nearly his hairline.

That look was very familiar to her. He'd used it often enough when she didn't hop when he told her to. She watched in stunned silence as the big detective reached in his pocket, pulled out the key, and unlocked her cuffs. She took a much needed breath and glanced at Nick. He looked furious.

"Morgan, these men said that you confessed to the murder of Alex Denty. Could you please tell them how you killed him? It's important that you give them as much detail as possible."

Morgan looked at Devin and realized the gig was up. He knew she didn't do it.

"Ms. Becky, we found some of your, hummm...some of your personal items at his house. There were several pair of your panties and a book," Detective Brownville said.

The detective had been so gentle with her earlier that she had broken down in tears when he told her he didn't believe her capable of killing a man Denty's size. He'd patted her hand and said the stupidest things to her while she sobbed.

"How do you know they were her panties? They could have been anyone's. And as for the book? Why, I probably have several hundred in my apartment right now," Nick said heatedly.

"They had her name in them and an ID number. They'd been scorched, the panties anyway. The book had been mutilated, but still readable."

"They were white?" At his nod, she continued. She knew where he'd gotten them. "I'd only been out of prison for a few days when my things were torched at the halfway house on Brendan. I think the police were called during an altercation. I was taken to the hospital with Dr. Grant. My things... I'd had a fight with one of the people there and she, Big Martha, claimed she was going to get me and got to my things first. I was approached by Denty in the hallway here. He...he told me that he'd like to...he wanted me to perform oral sex on him. I refused. He...he grabbed me when I came out of the bathroom a few minutes later and hit me. I must have fallen or something. The next time I woke up, I was being treated for injuries I didn't have before." She looked down at her hands. There were bruises forming on her wrist from her fighting with the cuffs.

"You and Dr. Grant, you were seeing each other? That why he came to the..." the detective started.

"I'm not seeing Dr. Grant. None of the Grants. I...I don't know why he was there at the halfway house. Stupid schmuck almost got himself seriously hurt. It ended up that he...he, ah, got in the way of my foot and I took him down. He was waiting for me to come out and talk with him when Big Martha attacked him," she said hastily.

"I see. Then what happened? Why did you kill him? I understand that he accosting you in the ER was bad, but why did you wait five months to murder him?" Detective Brownville asked.

She didn't look at anyone in the room for several long, tense seconds. For as much as she wanted to be guilty of this, she knew she couldn't lie.

"On Saturday evening, I was leaving my place to deliver some work site proofs to another client. I do web site creations for clients who want to expand their...never mind. Denty was waiting outside the building behind Mick's. I...he was in his cruiser, just sitting there. Him and another man I didn't know. I'd like for Dr. and Mr. Grant to leave, please. I don't think... They don't need to know what I did." She had been stupid when she hadn't reported him the first time she'd been attacked.

"We aren't going anywhere, Morgan. Finish the story. What happened next?" Nick sat down on her bed as he talked to her and took her hand in his. She looked down at them and didn't look up as she spoke.

"He and the man got out of the cruiser and approached me. I didn't say anything to either of them, but tried to go on my way. I don't move as well as I did before and Denty trapped me hard against the wall. He...please go away," she begged Nick softly.

"Go on, Morgan. He what?" Nick said.

"He groped me and pinched my breasts. I've learned not to fight him. It just seems to...to excite him more." She looked up at Nickolas to see how appalled he was at her behavior. She looked away quickly at the anger she saw there. *Well, why wouldn't he be?* she thought. She wasn't anything more than a slut to him.

"He told me that he was going to make me take him in my mouth that I was going to give him the best blow job I had ever given. The other man came up behind him and started to grope Denty from behind. When Denty switched me around so that the other man could come up behind me, I slammed my knee hard up into Denty's groin. When he doubled over, I grabbed his gun out of his belt and jerked away from both men."

Morgan lay back against the pillows behind her and looked at the couch again, seeing nothing but the scene reenact itself in her vision.

"Denty smelled of beer and sweat; the other man smelled of cigarettes and bourbon. I screamed at them to stay away, but as I took a step back to get away, I stumbled and nearly fell. The gun dropped from my hand and they attacked as one. I don't know how long they beat on me. I just curled myself into a ball to protect my belly. When I woke up, it was dark. Someone came along not too much longer. The rest you know."

Morgan pulled the sheet up over her shoulders and never looked up. She waited for them to say something, anything.

"Can you describe the man? I can have a sketch artist come in and have you work with him," Detective Brownville said gently.

"Would you like his picture? I took it with the cell phone that fell out of his pocket. I just kept pushing the little silver button on it. They didn't know I had it or I'm sure they would have taken it.

I had it hidden and took them while I was on the ground. I don't know if they're any good. I don't... I've never had one before, so it could be for nothing." No one said anything so she turned around and looked at Devin and the other two men. They were all staring at each other oddly. "Or not. I don't care if you take them or not. Besides, I'm sure the battery is dead by now."

"Where is it? The phone, where is it?" Detective Carol snapped at her. She flushed with embarrassment.

"Look, detective, she's cooperating. The least you can do is be polite. In fact, I demand that you be polite, or I pull the plug right now, and see where that gets you," Devin told the man.

"Are you threatening me? Because I don't take well to being threatened by anyone. Especially a two-bit lawyer that is—"

Morgan limped between the two arguing men and went to the little cabinet that held personal things for patients. She dug around until she found her pink bag and hauled it back to the bed. When Nick started to protest about something, she just glared at him and continued her search.

"Ms. Becky, please just tell me where it's at in there and I'll get it out.We would like to keep the fingerprints down to a minimum, all right? I have an evidence bag here that I'll put it in." *Oh*, she thought as Detective Brownville explained what he needed. *Of course, fingerprints.*

Morgan stepped back from her bag when she'd located the phone and let him retrieve it for himself. She could see her blood on it, along the front of the screen and on the silver button too.

"I didn't think to turn it off. To be honest, I never thought about it again until just now."

"You want to tell me now why you claimed you killed Denty, Ms. Becky?" Detective Brownville asked her while he sealed the little baggie. He was writing on it while she gathered up her things and her answer. No one was going to like what she said, she thought, and just blurted it out.

"I'd like to go back to prison as soon as this is born. I liked it there. I didn't... I fit in; it was safe and uncomplicated."

CHAPTER THIRTY-SIX

"You can't be serious. You *want* to go back to prison? Who in their right mind... You are certifiable, did you know that?" Nick could not believe anyone would want to go back to prison.

"I am not certifiable, you arrogant ass. I'm a realist. I can't live here. I don't understand people. I can't even raise a... I want you to get out of my room. I've had enough of you today." He watched as she struggled to get up on her knees and move toward him on the bed.

"I'm not going anywhere until we get this resolved. You are *not* going back to prison. Final."

Morgan was close enough now that he could see her eyes. They were darker because of her anger. They sparkled with fire and emotion. He suddenly had an overwhelming need to kiss her. To pull her mouth to his and take, to taste her again. He suddenly stepped back from her and she stumbled forward. He had to steady her, or she would have fallen off the bed and onto the floor.

Nick didn't want to get involved with her. Not now, not ever. She could be carrying anyone's child. Even his, but he didn't... He couldn't deal with that right now.

"I have to go. I have to be...I have to go." Nick was stammering and stumbling as he made his way to the door. He didn't even turn around and look at his brother as he made his way out. He'd almost kissed her.

After he left her room, he wandered around until he ended up leaving the building and along Maple Avenue toward the mall. Nothing was open this early in the morning, but he moved along the sidewalks just thinking. He turned back to the hospital after a few miles of wandering aimlessly.

What if she was carrying his child? Then what? Should he marry her, give in to her tricks? They didn't seem to even like each other most of the time, so he wasn't sure how that would work. Of course, that could be a part of her plan too. Marry then file for divorce, taking him to the cleaners. And what about his brothers and their proposals? Would she accept one of them over him? But he didn't think they were tricks. The more time he spent with her, the less and less they seemed like tricks and more like she was—

"Dr. Grant?"

Startled out of his musings, Nick turned toward the voice and saw Libby Sugar standing in the shadows behind him.

"Yes. Is there something wrong?" He realized that the sun had started to rise while he'd been sitting there. Pulling back his cuff to see his watch, he realized it was almost six-thirty.

"Your brother Damon asked me to take you to Devin's office. He's been detained on another emergency. Would you be all right with that?"

Shit, it was time. "Ah, yes, I guess that'll be fine. Anytime you're ready is fine with me." He stood up and stretched out the kinks in his back and shoulders. He'd been sitting there for nearly two hours and was no closer to figuring out what to do than before.

Forty-five minutes later and they were seated in Devin's

office waiting on the results. His entire family had shown up to wait, with the exception of Damon. He'd just called to say that he was on his way.

Nick didn't know what to think about that. They would all be supportive, but to whom, he didn't know. His mom was still upset with him, he knew, and Damon was barely speaking to him. He was standing next to the window, watching the rain pelt the pane, when he saw Damon pull into the parking lot below him. *The gang's all here.*

As Damon slammed his door shut and was darting to the front doors, the courier service pulled up too.

"They're here. The service just pulled up out front. Damon is here too," Nick told the room in general. His belly suddenly took a slight jump. Then he started rubbing his chest again. Christ, he could be a father in the next twenty minutes, he told himself.

Devin had asked him how he wanted the information. He had his choice of having it read by Devin in private, or Nick himself could read it in private, or Devin could read it to everyone. Nick really didn't know. He wanted all of them to happen at the same time. Privately with his family while Devin read it to him while he was still at home.

The courier handed the clipboard to him to sign, and once he had, handed the envelope to him. Nick sat down with it and didn't say a word.

Without looking at anyone in the room, he opened it and pulled out two sheets of paper. The first one was a table with rows and columns on it. Nick looked at it for several seconds and looked up as Damon walked over to him. He handed it to him. He didn't know what he was looking at anyway. The second sheet was an explanation.

RESULTS OF DNA ANALYSIS

Interpretation: Based on the DNA analysis submitted, the alleged father NICKOLAS PATRICK GRANT is the biological father of the twin unborn male children of MORGAN BECKY because they share the same genetic markers.

Combined Direct Index: 17,446
Probability Percentage: 99.9942%

Nick's first thought was, *I'm the father*; his second was, *twins*. He was the father of Morgan's twin baby boys. His and Morgan's twin baby boys. Father. He was a father.

"They're mine. Morgan's sons are mine." He was sure his family was saying something, but he couldn't hear over the loud buzzing in his head. The only thing he could understand was, "Twins, Morgan, Mine." It kept a constant loop going around and around in his head.

Nick didn't know how long his mom had been saying his name when she was suddenly in front of him. She was grinning. What the hell was there to be happy about? he thought.

"I said, are you going to go and talk to Morgan? She must be excited. Twins. And boys too. There haven't been twins born in our family in a few generations."

"She doesn't know she's carrying twins, or sons. She doesn't know anything about her babies other than their health," Libby Sugar said as she sat down across from him on the little, dark blue love seat.

"What do you mean she doesn't know? How is that even possible?" Nick asked her. Morgan was too thin, he realized. Much too thin to be carrying twins and be almost seven months pregnant to boot.

"She doesn't...no that's not right. She feels she can't get attached to the babies. She's not keeping them. And as for not knowing, she couldn't afford an ultrasound so none was ever preformed on her. She's been barely making it every month with just paying for the doctor and hospital bills in advance," Libby said. He watched as she pulled out a sheet of paper with neat columns on it. "The doctor demanded that she pay up front for his services. Let's see, that's about eleven thousand dollars. And as she doesn't have insurance, she's been making a payment every month to a special account to pay the hospital with when she delivers."

"Is that why she's so thin? She's not eating to pay the bills?" How could she jeopardize her health like that? Why the heck wasn't she asking for help? That sobered him. Why should she ask for help? She had to know he wouldn't have given it to her.

"No, she's thin because Simon had her on a three thousand calorie a day intake. He told her he didn't like his women to put on too much weight at delivery. He was about to lower that to twenty-five hundred because she'd had too much of a gain last month. He'd never checked for multiple births, and as she couldn't afford the 'extras,' as he called it, he'd never tested her." Damon sat down next to Libby on the love seat.

"Is that common practice, to have women eat so little during pregnancy?" Nick asked. He stood up and began pacing the room. He just happened to glace over at Damon when he realized he was rubbing his chest. Damn it, he was under a little pressure here, he thought.

"No, actually, it's very unsafe for both the mother and the baby. In Morgan's case, babies. Morgan isn't all that big anyway. If she makes it to full term, she'll be grossly underweight and may be too weak to deliver on her own," Damon told him.

"*If*? What do you mean if she makes it to term? You won't let anything happen to her, will you?" He watched as Damon looked over at Libby. "What's going on? What's happening with

Morgan?"

"I'm no longer her doctor as of you reading that letter. She went back to Simon this morning."

"Damn it! What is wrong with her? Does she want to die?" Nick sat down again. Hard against the seat and back. Did she? Neither Libby nor Damon would look at him directly. "Mother fuck!" he shouted.

After getting Devin's car keys, he took off back to Zanesville. It was high time him and his little mother-to-be had a long, serious talk.

~~~

"No, please, don't hurt me again. I hurt so badly now." Morgan had to get away before he caught her. Her legs ached and pulled. Something was wrong with her, something bad. If he caught her, he'd kill her. She could see the light ahead, the tiny pinhole of light. She opened her eyes.

Hospital room...she was back in the hospital room. When she had blinked enough, she realized that Nickolas Grant was sitting on the little couch and staring at her oddly. She glanced at the clock on the wall and saw that it was nearly eleven-thirty. He knew about the baby. Morgan felt along her bed sheets, found the pull for the nurse, and pulled gently on the cord.

"Morgan? Are you all right?"

She ignored him. No, she wasn't all right. She was seven months pregnant and in the hospital, stupid schmuck.

A nurse pushed open the door a few seconds later and walked in on them. Morgan still hadn't acknowledged him when he greeted the nurse politely. She did, however, smile for Shannon.

"Hi, Dr. Grant. Morgan, whatcha need?" she asked her.

"I need to go to the bathroom, please. And get a shower." She started to straighten out her gown and fuss with the sheet. She'd had a bad dream and had soaked them through with sweat.

"All right, but try to only stand up for five minutes. You remember what the doctor said. Stay off your feet as much as possible."

She nodded. She knew what Damon had told her. He'd said to stay off them altogether, but she was no longer his patient.

When she stood up next to the bed, she swayed heavily. Her vision blurred and she had to quickly lean back against the bed. If Shannon hadn't been holding on to her, she would have fallen in a fat heap on the floor. Morgan saw Nick move to her side, but she didn't, no, she couldn't look at him right now.

"You don't need a shower that bad. Get back into bed before we have to pick you up off the floor. Stupid woman, don't you know the meaning of the words too much?" he said.

Morgan would have laughed at the look of pure shock on Shannon's face at his words if she hadn't been trying so hard to stay upright.

It took her all of an hour to get to the bathroom and bathe. She hadn't had the energy to shower, so Shannon helped her take a quickie bath. It felt good to lie in the water and relax. Especially after getting to wash her hair for the first time in two days.

When she came out of the bathroom, Nickolas was still in the room. As Shannon was helping her back to the bed, he walked over. Actually, she thought it looked more like stalked over, scooped her up into his arms, and deposited her on the fresh bed. Even as she squeaked with indignation, he already had her put down and himself on the couch again.

Giggling loudly, Shannon left them alone again. She didn't have the energy to deal with him, so she rolled to her side away from him and put the sleeper to her cheek, rubbing gently.

Shannon had found it just this morning. It had gotten wound

up in her blankets when she'd been taken down to the x-ray room yesterday. She had been so happy she cried for nearly ten minutes.

Morgan was just closing her eyes when she heard a chair being moved across the room. Apparently, he didn't like being shut out. She didn't care and started to close her eyes again.

"I want to talk to you about our children."

Oh, now they were... Her eyes popped open and she stared at him. *Children*? As *in more than one*? He didn't say another word. She knew he had to know she didn't know about the children. Damon would have told him she didn't have any information about the baby, or babies, she guessed now. She closed her eyes again and realized what Shannon had meant when she'd said she needed to buy another one, another sleeper. Sons, they were twin boys.

"Okay, I'll talk and you'll listen. Starting right now, you'll eat as much as you want. No, let me amend that, you'll eat as much as Damon tells you to eat. Every day, Morgan. As soon as you're released from the hospital, you'll live in my house with me. I have several servants there that will see to your every whim when I'm not there. Someone will take you to your doctor's appointments and you'll follow the doctor's orders to the letter. I'm very serious in this." She thought he was finished with his rules, but apparently, he was saving the best for last. "And as soon as it can be arranged, we'll be married."

Morgan didn't even open her eyes or say a word. He could say whatever he wanted, about whatever he wanted, but she was a grown woman. There were long minutes of silence. Too long, she guessed later. It wasn't long until she was sound asleep.

CHAPTER THIRTY-SEVEN

When Nick woke up, he was alone in the room. There was a faint light coming from under the bathroom door and he assumed that Morgan had gone back to the bathroom. He stood up and stretched and realized it was full dark out. He must have slept the full day away. He actually felt pretty good.

Nick walked over to her bed and groped around for the light switch for the lights on the back of her bed. The sudden light illuminated the entire room and he immediately knew something was wrong. Shit! She was gone. He went to the nurses' station to ask where Morgan had gone.

"Can you please tell me when Morgan left? I was supposed to take her home with me, but I must have fallen asleep." Damned girl, he was going to strangle her when he found her.

"Dr. Grant? She left you a message." Nurse Fist handed him an envelope, went back behind the long counter, and flopped, no other word for it, back into her chair and went back to playing solitaire on the computer.

Dr. Grant,

I hope you enjoyed your nap. I've gone home. I don't want anything from you.

Morgan Becky
P.S. You snore.

Yes, when he found Morgan Becky, he was going to strangle her good. But first, revenge. Smiling, he left the hospital and made a few phone calls.

"Mom, its Nickolas. I need your help. Morgan is refusing to marry me and I was wondering if you could please go over to her apartment and talk some sense into her for me?"

"Of course. Why is that silly girl refusing to marry you? You're a good catch, and my grandbabies need a father. Not to mention the last name of Grant. I'll go over there first thing tomorrow." *Oh yeah*, he thought. *Revenge is going to be so sweet.*

"Not too early. I'm on my way there now, and I want to talk to her. Tell her what's going to happen with our future." He was hoping that anyway.

His next call was to his brother Devin. He wanted to make sure there was no way Morgan was going to be implicated in the murder of Denty. And that she would never see the inside of a prison cell again.

"No, she won't. Those pictures she took did the trick. The man's name who killed Denty is Marty James. He's an ex-cop on the police force from somewhere out West. He and Denty go way back and were lovers at one point." He could hear the hesitation in his voice. There was more.

"Tell me. I'm on my way to Morgan's house right now. The little imp left the hospital even though I expressly told her not to."

"She doesn't strike me as the type to just obey without question. If it matters at all, Nicky, I really like the girl." He stopped and leaned against the car.

"Yeah, it does. I like her too. Of course, I want to choke the girl most of the time, but I think I really like her."

"There are two minutes of video on the phone she recorded when she was pushing buttons." He was quiet for so long, Nick was afraid he'd lost the call and started to pull the phone back to check when Devin spoke again. "Nicky, what she endured...what they did to her was so much more than she told us. I...you should see it. I've been a criminal lawyer for a long time now and I was... No person, especially not a woman, should go through what she did. Ever."

Nick didn't want to see the video; he didn't even want to think about it. But he needed to be able to help her. "I'm going to go get a few things from my apartment and then go get a few things here in town. I need you to get my house opened up and ready for us sometime tomorrow. I'll meet you here tomorrow and see it then, all right?"

They agreed to meet at Muddy Misers in the old Putmun district. It was his favorite restaurant in this area, and served the best ribs in all of Ohio as far as he was concerned. He hoped Morgan thought so too.

Nick thought about her on the way over to his apartment. He'd treated her badly from the very beginning. When he thought about the night he'd...he hadn't made love to her, but had basically raped her. And had created children by that act. He knew that now. Hell, he'd known it then. He wondered if she'd ever forgive him. He wasn't sure he could forgive himself.

While he was at his apartment picking up a couple of changes of clothes, he called his good friend Thomas Shane. Thomas owned one of the most prestige jewelry chains in all of the Eastern part of the United States, and he lived right here in Zanesville. He made arrangements to meet him at one of the local branches in half an hour.

By the time Nick arrived at Morgan's apartment, it was after midnight. He thought about taking a room for the night and seeing her first thing in the morning, but every light in her apartment was ablaze so he went to the back entrance. The bar was still open for business and the noise was horrendous. His children wouldn't be living here, that was for sure.

He rapped twice on the door and waited for her to answer. He looked around the small area behind the bar and thought it was a nice and peaceful. Someone had put in a small koi pond and there were several chairs sitting around the entire wooded area. There was a large chimney pot sitting on a bricked part of the patio with a stack of small cut wood sitting next to it. There were potted plants, flowers of every color and hue one could imagine crammed in and around everything. On a cool night like this in early June, he could just see the two of them sitting together in the swing under the large maple a few feet from the pot. He was still smiling when Morgan opened the door. But it faded quickly when he saw that she'd been crying.

"What's happened?" He started to step into the room when she pressed her hand into his chest to stop him.

"Go away. Why do I have to keep telling you that? Is it just too much for your simple mind to comprehend? Here, let me help you understand. Then, next time, because I have no doubt there will be a next time with you, you may just leave when I say it. Go, as to leave behind, go away—to move along; travel; proceed. Away, in another place, in another direction—be gone. Understand? Good, good-bye." She almost had the door shut again, but he was just a little quicker.

Without thought to what he was doing, he cupped his hand behind her head and pulled her to his mouth. Heaven, he was tasting heaven and he didn't know if he ever wanted to give it up.

She was stiff and rigid, not yielding to him at all. But as he pulled her body to his, he felt her lean into him slightly at first, then more as the seconds passed. He captured her moan in his mouth, tasting her as she opened to him, for him. Stepping more in the room, he moved her, shifted her around until she was nearly back against the opposite wall, him pressing against her.

He could feel every curve of her body, including her belly hard against him. Her belly, swollen with his children, their children. He reached down and ran his hand across her mound and felt the first kick against his hand and at his groin. Before he could register what he'd felt, he was doubled over in pain.

"Ah, Morgan ..." was all he could manage as he fell to the floor. Damned woman had kneed him hard.

~~~

Morgan couldn't believe he'd shown up. But then when he'd kissed her, she didn't know what to think. For that matter, how to think.

He'd been lying on the kitchen floor for nearly ten minutes now. About five minutes ago, she'd taken him in a cushion from the couch and a blanket from the bed. She couldn't shut the door completely because he was still hanging half in and half out of it. She didn't want him to freeze while he was laying there. Stupid, arrogant dickhead. What was he doing here anyway?

Morgan looked up as, a few minutes later, he staggered in the part of the room she'd set up as her office. When he first showed up, she'd been finishing up on Byron's site. He'd startled her out of her zone when he'd knocked. She almost hadn't answered it, thinking it was the Sugars again, but looked anyway. Now, looking at him, she wished she hadn't.

"That wasn't playing fair. Kicking a man there hurts worse

than anything known to man," he said as he fell onto her couch.

"Oh, well, next time, I'll pull out a gun and shoot you there. Maybe it won't hurt you so much, but I'm betting your recovery time is a lot longer. What are you doing here at twelve-thirty in the morning anyway?" She looked down at her screen when the noise alerted her that the program she was loading was finished. She clicked on the next part of his site and ran it.

"I told you that you're coming home with me. Since you seem to like it here better, I've decided to move in with you. I brought some of my things. I'll have the rest brought over tomorrow sometime." He nodded toward the garment bag and suitcase just inside the door to her apartment.

"Oh no, you don't. There's barely enough room in this place for me and my stuff. You are not moving in here too." She stood up, but too quickly, and had to grab the table for support. He was there in a flash. And before she knew it, he had her scooped up in his arms and was sitting on the couch with her in his lap.

"Sit still before I paddle your butt. You know, you need a keeper. What would you have done if you'd of fallen on your face and hit your head?"

"It's a stupid question since I wouldn't have been getting up because you wouldn't be here to aggravate me. Let me go, you pigheaded swine." She struggled harder to get off his lap. In her haste to move, she inadvertently realized he was aroused. She stopped and looked at him.

"Sit still, Morgan, or we won't be going anywhere for a very long time. I want to talk to you." His voice was huskier and harder.

Well, she hadn't meant to do anything to him. Morgan blushed all the way to her toes. Men could be turned on by the weirdest things, she thought. "I want you to let me go. I don't...

188   *Kathi S. Barton*

just let me sit over there and I'll listen to you." For several seconds, she didn't think he was going to let her. He moved his arms from around her and she scrambled to the other side of the couch, as far from him as she could get.

"You're having my children, Morgan, and I don't want them raised by strangers. I want us to raise them." Of course he would. His family would do a good job of it too, she thought. She'd seen them all with Meggie. She knew they'd love these too.

"I don't know what that has to do with you moving in here. If you want to adopt them, then all right, I guess. There were only a few stipulations to the adoption I wanted. I don't think you'll have a problem with that."

"How much? How much to adopt my own children, Morgan?" His voice had changed again. She looked at him sharply. He was angry. Well, so was she.

"Money. It all boils down to money with you, doesn't it? If anyone wants anything from the exalted Nickolas Grant, there must be a monetary gain for them, right? Well, fuck you. One million dollars. You give me one million dollars and I give them to you, no strings. Now that we have that settled, I want you to get out. And stay out. If you come near me again before the deal is closed and you have your children, then I will put them on the black market and you'll never see them again." She got up, went to the door, opened it, and waited for him to go. Her heart was crushed and she was barely holding onto her tears and anger. When he picked up his things and walked out the door, she closed it quietly and clicked the lock.

Walking back to the living room, she sat down where he'd been sitting, pulled the little blue sleeper from her pocket and burst into tears, sobbing into it.

CHAPTER THIRTY-EIGHT

"You sure you want to do this? It doesn't seem all that smart to me, especially coming from you." Devin had been arguing with him for nearly two days about the money to Morgan. Devin wanted to set it up as a trust for her, given to her as soon as Nick had the babies. But Nick had his own ideas.

"No, this is how I want it. Those are the terms I want, and she'll either abide by them, or I'll sue her ass. I'm tired of fucking around with her." And he was too.

"You know that by you marrying her, she'd be able to receive alimony from you when you divorce. Because the way you two fight, it could only end that way or death for one or both of you."

"She's the one who wanted the million. She'll have it. But on my terms. You have the house ready for her?"

"Yes, it's in her name, along with the checking account and car. Nicky, if she didn't hate you before this, she certainly is going to now."

Nick didn't care how much she hated him. In fact, he relished the idea of her hating him. If she hated him, then she couldn't pull him back into her web. And maybe he could get over this obsession to be with her. He wanted things he'd never…things he had never thought to have.

Nick frowned when he thought about her asking for the money. Well, he thought again, she hadn't asked for anything. He'd asked. He could still see the look of hurt on her face when he'd asked her how much. But it was an act; he knew it was.

"Just make sure she signs the contact as soon as possible. I want to get things ready on my end and ensure that everything is ready for my sons." He walked out of Devin's office and up to his own. Without speaking to the new secretary, he went into his office to start his day. He'd been missing too much work lately and needed to get things back on an even keel again.

"Dr. Grant, your mother is on line one," the disembodied voice said over the intercom on his desk. He'd been sitting there for nearly an hour and he hadn't even signed into his computer. Shit.

"Hello, Mom. What's going on?" He'd been avoiding her too since leaving Morgan's house. He'd just remembered to call her and tell her not to go to her house just as she was pulling up in front of Morgan's apartment that morning. He'd only told her that he no longer needed her to persuade Morgan to marry him; he'd worked out an alternative solution.

"I want you to meet me for lunch today. I'll see you at Bergen's at one o'clock." He could tell by her voice that she was upset about something, but decided not to ask.

"I have other plans that I—"

"Perhaps I didn't make myself clear. I didn't ask you to meet me, Nickolas Patrick. I said to meet me. And you had better not be late." And then she hung up.

Nick knew he was in deep trouble if she was using his middle name as well as his first full name. He tried to think about what he'd done, and the only thing he could think of was Morgan.

She'd called her.

Looking at the clock on his wall, he realized he had about an hour before he had to meet his mom, so he called Damon. He knew that Morgan had a doctor's appointment today at ten and he wanted to know if she'd shown up and what was going on.

That same morning after leaving her apartment, he'd had Devin draw up a temporary contact with her stating that she would see the doctor of his choice from now on. It had taken him the better part of a day to convince Damon to take her as one of his patients. Morgan had given Damon permission to give Nick any information he wanted about her pregnancy, so he was invoking his rights by calling.

"It's Nick, did she show up?" Tansy had answered the phone when he'd called and when he told her who he was, she seemed less than happy to speak to him. Tough.

"Hello, to you too. Yes, she was here. I did a thorough exam and the babies are fine. She gained three pounds, which is normal this late in the second trimester. Their heartbeats are normal, and they are very active," he told him.

"How did she look? Is she eating? I mean, I read that the babies will gain weight whether there is sufficient intake from the mother or not." He'd been reading a lot too. Damon had given him four books and he'd bought nearly all the ones he could find at Borders Books.

"I can't tell you that. The babies are fine. They appear to be gaining weight and are active." Something was off. The last time Morgan was in his office, he had gone on for hours about her health, blood pressure, and her ankles swelling.

"What do you mean you can't tell me? It's a simple question. Is she all right?

"I mean I can't tell you anything about Morgan. I can give

you any information you want about the infants, but according to the contract she has with you, you aren't to get any more than that. I kinda like it too. So, you can threaten me all you want. But that's the way it goes from now on."

Nick realized that Damon was enjoying this. Damn it all to hell. Why did his family like her better than they did him? He knew the answer to that. Because he was being an ass.

"So you're telling me that if her ankles were swollen up to five times their normal size, you wouldn't tell me?"

"Nope. Not unless it was going to harm the babies. Then I'd be obligated to tell you, sorry to say."

"Damn it, Damon, this is serious. Is she all right? I demand that you tell me if she's eating properly and is healthy."

Nick heard Damon laughing, braying actually, as the phone went dead in his hand. He'd hung up on him. His own brother had hung up on him.

Nick was five minutes early for his lunch date with his mom. Bergen's was busy, as they normally were on Fridays, but he had no trouble finding her. He kissed her on her offered cheek and sat down after she did.

"When are you marrying Morgan? I heard from her that you're setting the entire thing up. She was just to show up and shut up." His mother had always been one to cut right to the point.

"Ten o'clock tomorrow morning, in Judge Carlton's chambers. I didn't tell her she had to shut up; I merely suggested she hold her tongue. And I gave her a choice of wedding plans. She's the one who said she didn't care."

"Well, I'm going to be there. And you'll give her your grandmother's ring too. If you're going to go through with this farce, then you might as well go all out." She reached into her bag and pulled out the little jeweler's box and slid it across to him. He opened the box and looked at the ring that had been in his family for seven generations.

It was a round two carat emerald with six quarter cut diamonds surrounding it. The band itself was wide, nearly an inch, and made of twenty-four carat gold. Each Grant that gave it to his wife added another diamond to the set. Last time it was used, when his father had married his mom, he'd had to have a second band added to hold his diamond. The small band that accompanied it was still nestled in the box. Neither he nor any of his brothers had used the ring because his mother had simply refused to let them, telling them that their choice of women was wrong and she wouldn't let this ring be lost to some bimbo. Turned out, she was right to refuse. He wondered why she was letting him use it for Morgan.

"I can't give her this. She and I aren't marrying for anything other than purely selfish reasons. Giving her something that means so much love to one another would be a travesty. No, I have a ring already for her." He pulled his own box out of his jacket pocket and handed it to his mom.

This ring was vastly different than the one his mother had given him. It was also different than the one he'd gotten from his friend Thomas the other night. This one was a simple band of twenty-four carat gold and a single half carat diamond. He wasn't even sure of her ring size and had gotten the smallest one they had, not even taking the time to have the ring wrapped for her.

"Nicky, don't do this. Don't do this to her or yourself. Call this off. Please?" He wondered if Morgan had anything to do with this and decided that she hadn't. She wouldn't get her million if they didn't marry.

"I have to. She's being well compensated. Don't worry about little Miss Becky. She's going to come out smelling like a rose and on her feet for the first time in her life. She'll have money and lots of it. I'll have my sons. That's all that matters."

It occurred to him then that it did matter. It was beginning to matter a great deal. Pushing that thought away, he picked up his menu to order, trying not to think about the constant pain around his heart.

~~~

Morgan didn't have any female friends to help her with her dress, so she didn't dress up. She had purchased her first maternity top yesterday at Wal-Mart and was wearing it with a pair of nice maternity Capri pants she'd purchased at the same time. Her shoes were a pair of sandals that she'd had for some time. She just washed them in the sink and slipped them on. Her ankles hurt too much and she couldn't bend over to tie her shoes so she was glad for the simplicity of the ones she had on. Besides, it wasn't as if this was a happy occasion anyway.

Morgan arrived at the courthouse at nine-thirty and sat in the little alcove waiting for this dickship to show up. She smiled at the name she'd dubbed Nick with. She thought it suited him perfectly. She heard them before she saw them, and was standing when his entire family came around the corner. Meggie broke from her father and ran to her, arms wide open and a huge smile on her face.

Morgan went down on one knee to receive Meggie and her hug. It felt so good that Morgan didn't want to let go. Finally, Meggie pulled back and kissed her cheek. Morgan struggled to stand up and was nearly there when she felt a hand at her elbow. She turned to thank whoever it was, but her throat closed off at the sight of Nick all dressed up.

He'd worn a suit and tie, as had the rest of his brothers. She ducked her head down to hide the sudden tears and pulled away from him. Mrs. Parker hugged her next and told her how lovely she looked with her hair down. The truth was, she didn't have the energy to braid the long tresses and just left it down most of the time anyway. She didn't go anywhere, so what was the point?

"Let's get this over with, shall we?" Nick said gruffly.

As he nodded at Devin, he stepped forward and gave her the final copies of the contracts. She'd had a copy delivered to her yesterday by courier and Libby said it was right. She was to move into the house on Beckon Way right after the ceremony. She'd had her things picked up by a moving company just this morning and they were on their way to her new home. At least for the next few months anyway. There was also a new car in the garage and a live in nurse to care for her. She was going to go by the contract to the letter, nothing more, and nothing less.

As soon as she delivered the twins, the house, the car, and any money in the account was hers. The million dollars would be deposited into the same account within twenty-four hours after he left the hospital with his sons. Nick was taking care of all bills she'd incurred as the result of the pregnancy; everything else was hers.

Morgan signed all the copies and was given one to take home. Another was to be given to her lawyer, Libby. She didn't know what happened to the other two, but assumed that Nick got one, as had Devin.

The judge that was to marry them was a really nice elderly gentleman with gray hair and twinkling eyes. He asked her if she had any family to stand up for her before they started and she told him no. He nodded and stepped away from her and to the Grants. At five minutes till the hour, two people showed up to stand with her as family. Judge Carlson had called his wife Tess and she'd brought her sister Caroline along too. Morgan was so touched she had to excuse herself to go to the ladies room and compose herself. Tess followed and helped her pin a beautiful rose to her shirt that she'd brought from her own garden.

"Teddy said you didn't have any flowers either. I was working in the yard and had just cut this when he called. It'll be just lovely with your red hair and all."

So Morgan Becky became Morgan Becky Grant fifteen minutes later. The ring that Nick had brought for her didn't fit, so neither of them exchanged rings. She was fine by that, less she'd have to return it when this was over. But he assured her he'd get it resized and have it to her soon.

"I don't want it. Keep it, or take it back. I'm fine without it." She expected him to make a snide comment, and he probably would have too, but Damon stepped between them at the last moment and kissed her on the cheek, welcoming her to the family. They'd had their "vows" altered to suit their predicament, so the words "love," "honor," and "till death we do part" had been omitted.

Mrs. Parker asked her to have an early lunch with them. Thankfully, she'd not said celebrate. Morgan declined. She said she was tired and wanted to take a long nap before going to Columbus later that afternoon.

Morgan was getting into the taxi to go back to the apartment when Byron came out of the courthouse. He hugged her tightly for several seconds. By the time he pulled away, she was crying openly.

"I'm so sorry, baby. Will you ever forgive me?" he said to her. She'd delivered his site to him yesterday morning. She looked at him confused. "For telling Damon you were pregnant. Nick might never have known if I'd of kept my mouth shut."

"No, he would have anyway. I'm required by law to tell him. You have nothing to be sorry about, Mr. Grant. Things will work out, you'll see. And they'll be raised in a good home with opportunities that I never had. You'll see. It'll all be fine." She hoped so anyway. At least that was what she kept telling herself. With another hug, she was off.

CHAPTER THIRTY-NINE

By the end of June, Morgan was miserable. Her ankles were swollen to twice their normal size. Her body ached in places she'd never hurt in before and she was lonely. The only person she'd spoken to verbally was Mrs. Puck, the live in nurse. And Damon once a month. When the phone rang, she didn't even bother picking it up. She no longer checked the mail, nor did she bother with the door bell. Nothing came for her, no one called for her, and no one came to visit. She did, however, answer her emails.

Byron, true to his word, told everyone about her business, Pink Bag Creations. She had more offers than she had time to do. Of course, she didn't turn them down, but worked on every one of them, banking the money in a separate account every time someone paid their bill.

It amazed her how much the bank wanted to help her now that her name was Grant. Before, she was ready to beg them to open an account and now she had two checking accounts, one that Devin had set up and one that she used with her own money. And she had a savings account where she was saving money to live on once she left the area after the babies were born, knowing that there wasn't any way she could stay close and not see them.

"Mrs. Grant, the doctor's office called. Dr. Grant wants you to come in in the morning and have an ultrasound done. I'm to tell you that your husband will also be there." *Flipping great*, she thought.

Morgan had asked her not to call her Mrs. Grant several times and had simply given up. Morgan thought she'd been told to do it.

"All right, just please have him make the appointment for as close to noon as possible, please." She was having horrific morning sickness in her last trimester. Damon had told her it was normal, but not to let it get too bad. If she threw up more than twice a morning, she was to call him immediately. She hadn't had to yet.

Morgan went into the big bright kitchen and opened the fridge. She needed to make herself some dinner.

Mrs. Puck had been surprised when Morgan started cooking for herself as soon as she moved in a month ago. Morgan thought about the look of pure horror on the woman's face when she'd seen what Morgan was going to eat that first day.

It had been late in the afternoon and she was tired from the ride and just wanted to lie down again. She'd pulled a box of cereal out of the cabinet and made herself a large bowl of cornflakes.

"I was to cook you some dinner, Mrs. Grant. I'm sure I can do better than cold cereal. What would you like?" she'd asked her.

"This is fine. And you won't be cooking for me either. You're here as a nurse and not a maid. If you want something and I'm cooking, fine, I'll throw extra in, but in no way are you fixing me a meal. Understand? You are also not to do my laundry, clean this house, or do any outside yard work. This house belongs to me and I'll be responsible for it," Morgan told her.

"But Dr. Grant said I was to—"

"Dr. Grant doesn't live here. I do, and so do you as long as you abide by my rules of the house," Morgan said firmly.

"I'll have to clear this with Devin Grant. I'm sure that he is the one who set this up. You can bet he'll be none too happy about your arrangements." *Good to know*, she thought as Mrs. Puck stormed out of the kitchen.

After Morgan was finished eating and washing up the dishes, Mrs. Puck came in to say Devin Grant was on the phone for her.

"Morgan here, may I help you?" She couldn't bring herself to say her name was Morgan Grant. She wouldn't be keeping it after the babies anyway, so why get used to it?

"Giving him a run for his money is one thing; being stupid is quite another." She simply hung up on Devin and walked into the bedroom she was using. Ten minutes, later Mrs. Puck told her Devin was on the phone again.

"Morgan Grant, I am not my brother and won't —"

This time, she was in the bath tub when he called back.

"Okay, let's start over. I want to know about this arrangement you have with Mrs. Puck, please. She said that you only use her for medical reasons and won't let her do the things she was hired to do." His voice was a little hard, but at least he wasn't yelling at her.

"Was she hired as my maid, or was she hired as a live in nurse? Because, Mr. Grant, as you are well aware, I didn't agree to the first part."

"She was hired as both. She was told that she would do a little light cleaning and cooking in addition to making sure your...that you... She was hired primarily as a nurse."

She had to smile at his fluster. "You mean she's here to make sure that I don't harm the Grant twins? Then that's all she'll do. Is there anything else that you'd like to get cleared up while I'm still speaking to you?" He burst out laughing. *Good*, she thought, *keep them guessing*.

"No, Morgan, nothing else. If you need anything, please don't hesitate to call me."

Mrs. Puck pulled her from her musing when she cleared her throat. She looked at the woman and smiled. Mrs. Puck didn't approve of her, not her relationship with her "husband," or the way she ran the house, but she did respect her position. Morgan sat up a little straighter on the sofa and looked at her. Her feet hurt so bad that she didn't take them off the coffee table just yet.

"He said to tell you the best he could do was nine-thirty and the fridge is dead. It started making the funky noise again this morning, and it stopped. Now, it's not doing anything. The light won't even come on."

"All right, I'll call and have it replaced. Thanks for telling me. Aren't you supposed to be off tonight?" She and Morgan had come to an arrangement of sorts. Every other Thursday night, she would go out for the evening and Morgan wouldn't do anything too stupid.

"Just leaving. Want me to call Mr. Grant for you before I leave?" Yes, she did, but she knew that she should do it on her own.

"I'll do it, have fun." Morgan went to the kitchen and called the office of Grant, Attorney at Law while she looked in the fridge. *Yep, dead as dead can be.*

"Hi, this is Morgan. Could you please let Mr. Grant know that I've replaced the refrigerator and need to know what he wants done with the old one? He can call me back at his convenience."

"Mrs. Grant, he's free. Would you like to speak to him directly? If you wouldn't mind holding for a minute, I'll put you through." And before she could tell her no, she was being transferred. She actually thought about hanging up, and just before she did, he came on the line.

"Hello, Morgan? So the refrigerator died, huh? You have an account. Just order it and have the bill sent to the office here," he said to her in way of greeting.

"No. She didn't have to put me through. You told me to inform you when an appliance went bad. I have. So, I'll...good-bye, Mr. Grant." The phone was nearly to the hook when he yelled at her to stop.

"Morgan. My name is Devin. Please stop calling me Mr. Grant. I'm your brother-in-law, not some stranger."

Morgan leaned her head against the cabinet above her head. They were all strangers to her. She didn't want to be their friend, because it would hurt less when she stepped out of their brother's life.

"Morgan? Are you there?"

She wiped furiously at the tears. It seemed as though every little thing set her off nowadays. His voice was gentle and caring.

"Yes. I have an appointment soon. I have to...just email me with the place to have the dead refrigerator taken. I...good-bye." And she hung up before he could say anything else.

Twenty minutes later, she had a cheap replacement being delivered tomorrow. And they had agreed to take the old one and set it in the garage for her. Life was suddenly all right.

She was running late. Something she detested more than anything else. But she'd had a slight accident with her blouse and she'd had to change. She didn't think puke down the front of her would leave a good impression on her "husband." The taxi driver had been sweet; he'd even kept the car running so it would be cool when she came back out to get in.

By the time she'd paid him and was headed up in the elevator, she was thirty minutes late and had to be sick again. It was all the rushing around, she thought, and being off her schedule. Hurrying into the office, the nurse took one look at her and rushed her past the other patients and right to the employee bathroom.

She didn't have anything left in her belly so all she was doing was heaving when someone knocked on the door.

"Morgan, it's Nickolas, let me in." *Great, just frigging great.* She'd not seen him in five weeks and now that she was sicking up her breakfast, he wanted to chat.

"I'm a little busy right now. How about we meet later when I'm not quite so preoccupied?" Reaching over to the little sink, she turned the water on full blast. That did help with drowning him out, but now she had to pee. Again.

Nick was standing on the other side of the door when she opened it five minutes later. She supposed it was too much to ask that he go sit in the waiting room. Ignoring him as best she could, she went to the front desk and asked Tansy where they wanted her.

"I would like a word with you, if you don't mind? You look like hell. And I want to know why you aren't returning my calls."

"I do mind. I don't want to speak to you. But I will answer you. If I look like hell, it's none of your business. It has no direct correlation to the babies, so it's not anything to you. As for calling you back, you can ask me questions through my lawyer. Now, if you don't mind, I'm tired and hot and I want to sit down." She brushed past him and into the room that she was to be examined in.

Morgan had just put the paper gown on when Damon and Nick came in the room after a brief knock. Damon was smiling and Nick looked ready to bite a nail in two.

"Morgan, how are you doing? Need help getting up on the table?"

Damon always asked her the same thing, and she never answered. It was getting harder to "hop" up on the table, but she just managed it. Pulling the sheet across her waist, she watched as he measured her from groin to the top of her mound. Laying down like this, she felt like Mount Everest. Probably looked like it too. He measured, took notes, and made funny noises in the back of his throat. Nick watched everything he did like there was going to be an exam later and he didn't want to fail.

"You've gained six pounds this month. Not bad, not bad. I want to start having you come in weekly now. You're due date will change because of you carrying twins. I'd like to say you'll deliver around the tenth or eleventh of August. But as stubborn as you are, I've no doubt those boys will be too, so we'll shoot for then. I don't want you to go much past that because of your size and theirs. I'd also like you to curtail your standing time. How long would you say you're on your feet now?"

"I guess about ten hours at day. Sometimes more, but not much," she told him.

"Why are you on your feet so much? You should be sitting down or lying down as much as possible with your feet up above your heart," Nick interjected. They both ignored him.

"I'd like you to try to get that number down to half. Your due date is in less than six weeks, so I'd also like for you to carry a cell phone or be with someone whenever you're over a mile from home. I don't think anything will happen, but with twins, it's hard to know. Okay, Tansy will come in and help you to x-ray and we'll do that today. I'm a little concerned about the swelling, but we'll discuss that later."

She could hear Nick saying something to his brother as the door shut, but she wasn't really paying attention. Less than six weeks to go.

Tansy came in a few minutes later with a smile and a Snickers. Morgan nearly wept with happiness. It had become a ritual with them. She would get weighed and examined; Tansy would slip her a candy bar. This time, the chocolate was like ambrosia to her. Her stomach was empty and Nick was here.

Morgan waddled down the hall clutching her sheet around her like a toga. Her last two bites of her candy bar were the closest thing to happiness she'd had in a while. Nick popped out of the door just in front of her and nearly knocked her over. As he made a grab for her, the sheet slipped and he got a handful of her breast. Her very full, very tender breast. She moaned before she could stop herself.

Without waiting for the sheet to be pulled all the way back in place, she darted around him and into the room. She'd never been so mortified in her life.

The rest of her doctor's appointment was made in silence. Neither of them spoke to each other nor to Damon. When Morgan went to the front desk to make her next appointment Nick, was going in Damon's office.

"Morgan, are you okay? You seem...I don't know, distracted," the nurse making her next appointment asked.

Well, duh, she wanted to snap at her, but only nodded and left. She was married to a man who despised her, having his twin sons, living in his house, and had six weeks left in the only home she'd ever known. Nope, not distracted at all.

~~~

"Should she be that puffy?" Nick asked his brother as soon as the door shut to his office.

"Puffy? I don't know what you're referring to. Her ankles are swollen because she's carrying around extra weight and it's hot. The babies are fine. I don't see any problems with the delivery.

Boy one is head down and in a good position. Boy two is up, but that's nothing to be concerned about. He can flip or not."

"Is she going to be all right?" Damon looked at him for a long time. Nick had seen her belly—it was hard to miss—during the ultrasound. She was so big.

"The babies are fine, Nick. She hasn't done anything to harm your sons."

He wanted to scream. No one would give him any information about her. Not even her nurse and he was paying.

Nick left the office a short time later. He was no closer to knowing if she was going to be all right than he had before. She was his wife, for Christ's sake, and not one person would tell him anything about her. He glanced up in time to see someone who looked like her get into a cab. A cab. Why would she…? It would be just like her to not use the car he'd given her. Damned girl probably sold it.

A week later, he was back in his office and in a foul mood. He noticed that his receptionist was out to lunch. He thought she was out to lunch even when she was there, but he'd not replaced her yet. He'd been busy.

Nick picked up the phone to call Devin just as he walked in his office. He had Byron with him.

"Hi, did you know that your receptionist is a moron? I called up here earlier this morning to speak to you and she didn't have a first clue as to who I was asking about. I think you should fire her and find someone else. Soon." Devin plopped down in his chair.

"Yeah, I was just thinking the same thing. Want to go and get some lunch? I'm starved and I need a break." It was nearly one now, and he knew he was free the rest of the afternoon.

"Yeah, but I gotta…why don't I meet you there? I have

something I have to do later and it'll be easier if I drive my own car." Devin was hiding something. He'd always been bad at lying, which was the same as evading.

"Nah, we can go together. I'll wait for you while you take care of business. It's getting later all the time," he told him.

"Nicky, I have to go see Morgan. Something happened to the fridge last week and I didn't get a bill yet. She said she had to replace it and I wanted to make sure she's had one delivered. It'll be much smoother if you don't go." *Well, why don't you just be a little more blunt*? he thought.

"You talk to her? How often? And what do you mean you haven't received a bill? There's money enough on the credit card I set up for her; have her use it. That would generate a receipt you can use, wouldn't it?"

"Yes, there's plenty of money on the credit card for that and anything else, but, as far as I can tell, she's never used it. None of the money we've set up for her, as a matter of fact. I just want to go see if she got one, or do I need to be all manly and order her one?"

Nick looked at Byron when he snorted at them. "She wouldn't use it if her life depended on it. Just like she won't tell you any personal information. Just like she won't let you run her life."

"She is stubborn, I'll give her that. I've never met a more pigheaded person...well, never a more pigheaded female. The only other person I can think of who's more pigheaded is you." Devin pointed at Nickolas and smirked before continuing. "Probably why she thinks you hate her so much, I guess."

That stunned Nick. Hate her? Did she really think he hated her? She aggravated him most of the time to the point where he wanted to spank her, but hate her? He didn't hate her.

The men had a great dinner at Max and Erma's downtown

and had enjoyed teasing each other for nearly the whole late afternoon. Devin's phone rang a couple of times, but once he looked to see who it was, he simply put the phone away.

While Nick was paying the check, it rang again.

"Grant." Nick smiled at that. He knew it wasn't his mother this time. She hated when they barked their names in the phone. As he moved to go outside, he realized Devin was no longer with him. Just as he turned to go back inside, he came out.

"Where did you...what's happened?" Devin was visibly upset and tense.

"There's been a break-in at your house. The police can't tell me anything because they can't contact the owner. They've taken a female away in an ambulance, Mrs. Puck, I told them. He said that she wasn't pregnant, but... Nick, they can't find Morgan. She's not there. They can't find anyone else in the house. And Mrs. Puck is in surgery."

They were running to Nick's car as Devin filled him in. When they got to his SUV, he realized he couldn't drive. His body was going ninety miles an hour and he knew he couldn't get behind the wheel. He handed the keys over to Byron and slid in the front seat. Devin was still making calls.

They were only about twenty minutes from the house, but it seemed an eternity. When the vehicle pulled into the drive, Nick was out and up the front steps before either of his brothers were out of the car. *Morgan, Morgan, Morgan* kept running through his mind.

Nick tried to enter the kitchen, but was stopped by a young beat cop before he got within ten feet of the room. Devin and Byron were right behind him.

"I need to find my wife. Please, I need to see if Morgan is in there somewhere," he begged the cop.

"No one else is in there, buddy. We looked everywhere for her and she's not there. I'll go get my captain. He wants to talk to you. Just don't go in there; it's a crime scene and we can't have civilians walking all over the place. All right?"

Nick nodded. Crime scene. He couldn't mess up the crime scene. He sat down heavily in one of the chairs near the fireplace. His legs suddenly couldn't support his weight.

"Dr. Grant, are you all right?" He looked up at the man who was speaking to him. He didn't know who he was, but he was dressed like the policeman who was guarding the door.

"Morgan, my wife, have you found her yet? She's eight months pregnant with our twins. Please tell me she's all right."

"No, we haven't found her. I don't believe she's here. The woman, the nurse, she couldn't tell us anything yet. We received a nine-one-one call to this address from the security firm who monitors it. They couldn't get an answer when they received the alarm. Mrs. Grant has apparently set the alarm off once or twice since moving in, but they've always made contact with her right away. Someone forced their way in the back door and broke the glass. Mrs. Puck looks like she tried to fight her assailant, but he over powered her and broke her arm and her leg. Does your wife have a cell phone we could call? Maybe she's over at a friend's or something and doesn't know what's going on here," the policeman said.

"She doesn't have a cell that we know of, yet. She was to get one soon, though. I...the doctor told her she should carry one in case she was out and went into labor." The door behind them crashed open and in came his mom and Spencer, followed closely by Damon and Meggie. He reached for her and she wrapped her arms around him.

"Have they found her yet? That poor girl. I wonder what

happened to her. She'll be fine, Nicky, you'll see. She's just out and will be coming through that door any minute wondering what all the fuss is about. Why, she'll be yelling at you for being here and all the mess...oh, Nicky, I want her here." She started sobbing in his arms. He looked up at Spence and he came and pulled her into his arms and shuffled her to the couch.

The police went over every inch of the house, then when they were finished, they started over. Nick had followed them both times.

Nearly three hours later, his cell rang. He nearly ignored it, but answered the payphone call anyway.

"Grant. I don't really have time to talk right now, but I'll—"

"If you tell me that Mrs. Puck is all right then I'll hang up. I've been out of..." Morgan said, interrupting him.

"Where the fuck are you? You know that we've been trying to...she hung up on me." Nick looked at his mother as he said it. He'd been worried about her all day and she had the nerve to hang up on him.

"Yes, imagine that. If you were that snarky to me, I would have hung up too," his mom said to him.

He looked over at Devin as his phone started to trill. When Devin looked over at him, he knew it was a payphone call too.

He stood up and went to him as he answered.

"Hello, Grant here. Morgan?"

Nick put out his hand and waited for him to give over his cell.

"...so if you could just tell me how she is, then I'll come on home," she was saying.

"You'll fucking come home now. I've been waiting here... mother fuck! She did it again. I swear to Christ, I'm going to... ouch! That fuc...that hurt. What was that for?" He rubbed his ear where his mother had pinched him.

"You kiss me with that mouth, and I'll paddle you good, young man. You are not too old for me to get medieval on your buttocks, you hear me? Sit down!"

Nick sat. His mom had that look in her eye that terrified each and every one of his brothers and him. It said, "I brought you into this world. I will fucking take you out of it too." They all knew she would too.

"Yes, ma'am. But she hung up..." She cut him off with a look. He stared at her for a few seconds because he could swear that he'd seen that same look on Morgan's face a couple of times when they'd been fighting.

Nick tensed up when Byron's phone rang. He started to rise, but Mom just looked. Damn it, he was a grown man. He sat back down.

Nick watched as Byron causally pulled out his phone and winked at him. Payback was going to hurt him so bad. As if his mother knew what he was thinking, she glared at him again. Damn it all to hell and back.

"Hello, love. Are you all right?"

He waited for some news about her, anything would be good.

CHAPTER FORTY

"If he comes to the phone again, I swear I'll hang up and won't call back again. I'm out of change anyway, and phone numbers to call," Morgan told Byron. She should have just called him in the first place. But her first thought had been Nickolas.

"She said that if Nicky comes to the phone again, she'll stay where she is and have the babies on the street corner," she heard him tell the room.

"I did not! Are you trying to cause trouble? You are, aren't you? Good then. Is Mrs. Puck all right? I just heard about it on the news. Who did this, Mr. Grant?"

Morgan had been coming out of the bathroom when there was a news flash on the television. It had said they were looking for a man who had broken into her home and that she was missing. All she'd been able to think about was poor Nickolas. Well, she thought, that was stupid on her part. All he'd done was yell at her.

"Yes, love, she'll be fine. Her leg is broken and she's been sedated. She hasn't regained consciousness, but Damon said that's to be expected. You'd better tell me where you are before Nicky breaks my neck." Morgan burst into tears. She'd been doing that a lot lately and it was getting worse all the time. The stupidest things would set her off.

"I'm in Mansfield on a job site. I wanted to get the pictures before Dr. Grant won't let me travel anymore. I have a job doing a site for the Mansfield Prison. Isn't that wonderful? The only bus I could get back to Columbus is a milk run, some man called it, and we've stopped in every little town between here and there." She waited while he relayed the information, this time telling them what she said. Morgan felt silly crying and was glad Byron hadn't commented on it.

"Nick would like to know if you need someone to come and get you? He said that he could be there in an hour."

Alone in a car with Nickolas for an hour. No, and hell no. "No, I'll be nearly there by the time he gets here anyway. I'm tired and my back hurts. I just want to come home. I should be there by eight or eight-thirty. Tell everyone to go home and I'll call them tomorrow. I'd better hang up. I only have thirty-three cents left in change and that's not enough for another minute anyway. So, good-bye." And she hung up just as the recording was telling her to deposit another seventy-five cents to continue her call.

Morgan went to the little shop just inside the bus terminal and bought herself a juice and a candy bar. Just as she was leaving, she went back and purchased two more candy bars. She was starving and knew she had at least another hour and a half before she could fix herself anything to eat.

Getting on the bus wasn't easy. The steps were very high off the ground and she was so rotund. Once she settled back against the seat, she thought about her day.

Earlier, she'd met with Libby and finalized the paperwork concerning the money that was to be given to her when Nick's sons were born. There was also the house and the car. Everything would be in their names, once Nickolas named them. She hadn't wanted any of it in the first place, so giving it to her children—no,

Nick's children, she amended — was easy. As soon as the million dollars was deposited, it went directly into another account for them as well.

Libby didn't argue with her about it. Morgan fully expected her to. She'd even made a few suggestions on what to do about the car. But she felt that as she'd never driven it, Nickolas should be the one who disposed of it.

There was also the file of pictures she'd made for Byron. They were pictures of her in different stages of her pregnancy. Byron had taken most of them, but a few she had taken with the tripod as well. She'd written him a long letter about why she'd given him the file. If the boys ever asked about her, would he please show them how happy she'd been to be pregnant with them? And that her leaving them had nothing to do with them. It was all her fault that she couldn't make her marriage work with their dad. That their dad was a wonderful man and loved them very much.

The bus pulled onto the highway about ten minutes later and the gentle sway and the soft moonlight shining in the window soon lulled her to sleep.

~~~

The big Greyhound pulled into the bus station at eight forty-five. Nick watched every person who got off the bus, waiting for Morgan. He'd done a lot of thinking since she'd called and she'd been right to hang up on him.

Nick thought about every time they'd been together and how very little they had talked. She would say something, and he'd bark at her. She'd ask a question, and he'd snarl at her. No wonder she avoided him as much as possible. He would too if he could.

When no one else seemed to be getting off the bus, he looked around the terminal. He didn't think he'd missed her, but she might have seen him first and darted away. If she could even dart anymore. Christ, she had been so big when he'd seen her last. He was just about to go look for her in the bathroom when the driver motioned for him. He walked over to the man and shook his hand.

"You looking for a woman, boy?" He'd not been called boy since he'd been a teenager.

"I don't need a woman, mister. I've got a wife. You shouldn't be selling women either. It's degrading and against the law." He started to walk away, but the man's next statement stopped him.

"I gots me a pregnant woman on this here bus who ain't woked up yet. I was wondering if'n you was awaitin' on her. Pretty little thing too. Looks ready to about pop if'n you asked me."

"Morgan's asleep. Yes, she's my...is she all right?" He moved past the man and onto the bus. He couldn't see her, so he turned back to the driver.

"'Bout half way back on the left. Be careful of her; she's been alying like that since we tooked off. She'll be all kinked up."

Nick went slowly to where he had indicated and found her just where he said she'd be. He kneeled down and looked at her breathing softly all rolled up in a ball. He leaned forward and pressed a kiss to her brow and she turned to look at him.

"Oh, Nickolas, I was having the most wonderful dream about us," she said dreamily. She started to move tighter into a ball and sighed heavily. "It's too bad it wasn't true. I love you so much." And she was asleep again.

Nick stopped breathing as he fell back against the floor of the bus. He felt...well, he knew what the term pole axed meant now. Morgan loved him.

Nick looked over as the driver came back to them. He couldn't think past her words. It was perhaps a few seconds before he realized the man was speaking again.

"...that way you won't have to carry her out to the parking lot. He said to just pull up out front of the terminal and he'll wave you through."

Nick was supposed to pull up out front. *Then what*? he thought. "I'm sorry, I...what did you say?" He wanted to shout, "she loves me!" but didn't think the man would understand.

"Hee hee, you love on that girl right and she won't be moving off again. Nah, she didn't tell me nothing, but I got eyes. I seen the way you looked at her. Go on now, get your car. I'll wait right cheer with her."

Nick didn't know how he got to his car, or how he was able to get around to the bus again, but was suddenly there again. True to his word, the driver stayed with her until he returned.

Nick gently picked Morgan up and lifted her to his chest. She was heavier than he'd remembered, then realized that the only time he'd had her in his arms was when she was in pain or hurt. She didn't stir much when he got her out of the seat and only moaned slightly when he put her into the passenger seat of the SUV. He was nearly halfway home when he realized he hadn't thanked the man for his help.

Nick took her to his apartment because the police wouldn't let them fix the door until they were finished with it. Parking in the garage was tricky because his parking place had a wall next to it on the opposite side and he couldn't get her out without banging her around. He ended up having the front desk move his car around to the garage while he brought her up through the front doors. Once he got upstairs, thanking everyone he could that he lived in the penthouse and keys weren't necessary to open his door, he took Morgan directly to his bed and laid her down on it. As gently as he could, he removed her shoes and socks. He debated on the rest of her clothes, but she'd be waking up in a strange room and he didn't want to frighten her anymore than necessary.

After he got her settled, he went into his living room and collapsed in his favorite chair. Morgan Grant, his wife, mother of his children, loved him. He knew he was grinning like a loon, but couldn't seem to help it.

The next thought sobered him up quickly. *But how do I feel about her?* Did he love her? He honestly didn't know.

Nick certainly lusted after her. Even as big and full as she was right now, he wanted her. But did he want to spend the rest of his life with her? Did his feelings for her make him want to wake up next to her every morning, go to bed with her every night? Did he want to spend time with her above all else? Sometimes, he thought. Other times, not so much. But she made him laugh. The unexpected bursts of laughter that surprised him when he did it. Did he love Morgan Grant? He didn't know.

Nick called his mom to tell her that he'd picked up Morgan at the terminal, and that she was with him.

"Nick, darling, try not to piss her off tonight. She's had a terrible day and she probably needs her rest. Why don't you sleep on the ugly couch of yours until tomorrow? That way you won't wake her and start anything this late."

"Good night, Mother. I'll talk to you tomorrow." He was still grinning when he went into his room to check on her.

Morgan hadn't moved. He started taking off his tie as he looked down at her in wonder. She was very beautiful. He pulled his shirt from his pants and unbuckled his belt. Toeing off his shoes, he thought about the children she carried and wondered if they'd look like her. He hoped that one of them would get her eye color. The sheer blue would be breathtaking on a young man as it was on his mother.

Nick sat down on the bed as he pulled his trousers off. As he tossed them across the room, he wondered if she would be hungry when she woke up. Damon had told him that she was having late pregnancy morning sickness. As he pulled the blanket out from under him and lay down, he thought he'd have to get up early enough to go get some things for breakfast for them. Maybe a few weeks worth of groceries because she wasn't staying in that house alone. He closed his eyes and pulled her lax body next to his. No, he thought. She wasn't staying anywhere alone again.

CHAPTER FORTY-ONE

Morgan woke up hot. Her body was drenched in sweat from her head all the way down to her feet. When she tried to move away from the source of heat, it literally pulled her back again. It was then that she noticed the huge arm across her just under her breasts. *OhGodohGodohGod*! Where was she?

Turning slightly, she got a whiff of aftershave and shampoo. Nickolas. Damn it, how had she ended up in bed with him?

Lifting his arm as gently as she could, she tried to slip out from underneath it. It was heavy and she wasn't in a position to move it high enough over her girth to raise up. She wanted to sit up and was nearly to the desperate point of needing to pee too.

Waking him up was the only solution. She began by shaking him gently. When that didn't work, she started rattling him as hard as she could.

"Morgan, if you don't stop beating on me like that, I'm gonna spank you." He didn't even open his eyes. Jerk.

"I have to pee, and I might be sick again. Let me up, hurry." She might have laughed at the speed he moved off her if she didn't have her own emergency just then.

Morgan barely made it to the toilet before she started throwing up. There wasn't much in her stomach, but it still made her ache to heave like this. When she felt she could manage it, she sat down to pee. Those seemed to be the only things she was getting really good at, peeing and heaving.

When she stood up to wash her hands, she noticed blood in her panties. She sat back down so abruptly that she banged her teeth together. Blood. Heart pounding and her head spinning, she tried to think past the noise buzzing in her head. It was no use.

Morgan needed to call Damon. He'd know what to do. Blood in her underwear at eight and a half months pregnant wasn't the end of the world. *Right*, she thought.

As she stepped out of the bathroom, she noticed that Nick was getting dressed. She must have made a small noise because he turned around to her.

"Morgan, what is it? You look like you've seen a ghost. Here, sit down. Have you ever noticed how much I'm asking you to sit down? You might want to think on that when you're scaring the life out of me like you are now."

"You never ask me to sit down. You're forever demanding that I sit, like I'm some sort of dog you're trying to paper train. Nickolas, I need to call Damon. Something is wrong. I...I have blood. Can you please dial it for me?"

Nick picked her up and pulled her into his lap. She couldn't see his face, but her head was resting on his chest so she could hear his heart beating fast.

"Honey, how much blood? A lot?" She shook her head no. There wasn't really, she supposed. "Okay, is it your mucus plug? You know, the barrier? It would be sticky and clear with blood tinged in it. Could that be what you saw?"

Morgan remembered something about that. Damon had told her that she'd lose it sometime in the last part of her pregnancy. She suddenly felt stupid. Of course that's all it was. She started to slide off his lap when he held her tight again.

"Please just sit here with me until my heart moves down into my chest again. Shouldn't be too much longer, ten or eleven years maybe."

She could hear his heart. It was just where it should be and it wasn't pounding like it had been before.

Nick's hand was resting on her thigh, she noticed. She wondered what he'd do if she picked it up and placed it over where his sons were currently playing football with each other. Just as she was going to lift his hand to put it there, someone pounded on the front door, startling both of them.

"I have to get that. I ordered some groceries to be delivered this morning." He didn't move. Neither did she. When the pounding came again, she moved off his lap and he stood up and moved toward the door. "Morgan?" She turned when he didn't finish. "I'll call Damon for you." And he left her.

Morgan decided to take a shower and wash her hair. She couldn't find her clothes and as much as she hated to bother his, she went to his closet and pulled out one of his darker dress shirts. Reaching into her bag, she found a clean pair of panties and a clean bra. Her under things were getting very tight on her, but she wasn't spending money on things she'd only wear for a few more weeks.

Before she stepped into the living room, she could hear someone talking. Nickolas, she could hear, but the other voice seemed farther away.

"Dr. G., I am not gonna fix a pregnant woman no breakfast without asking her if she can eat it. That would just be cruel and unusual. Maybe she don't be liking eggs. Ever think on that one? No, we'll just wait until she...hello there. My, aren't you a pretty little thing?"

Morgan actually looked behind her to see who the little thing was. She realized suddenly Mary Janis, Nickolas' cook and cleaning lady, was referring to her. Blushing hotly, she walked more into the kitchen. Nickolas was grinning at her like he was half crazed. Idiot man.

"I'd actually love some breakfast. I'm starving. I haven't eaten since yesterday afternoon. Well, except a couple of candy bars. I was gonna eat last night, but I don't remember getting home." She realized just then that she didn't even know how she'd gotten here. Looking around, she didn't even know where here was.

Morgan must have looked confused because Nick answered her musings. "This is my apartment. I picked you up at the bus station last night and brought you here. They wouldn't let us fix the door, and I couldn't leave you there alone, so here you are."

Breakfast was delicious. She didn't care for bacon, but there were sausage links and fried ham. Hot biscuits and hash browns, eggs, and fresh sliced tomatoes were also added to her plate. Morgan ate two helpings of everything.

"I think there might be a couple of hunks of old moldy cheese if you want it. I'm sure Mary could fry them up for you," Nick told her. She wasn't going to feel bad about it; she'd been very hungry and it was wonderful.

"I wish I would have found you sooner, Mrs. Janis. I might have stolen you away to come live with me." Nick looked at her oddly and she realized what she'd said and changed the subject. "Did you get in touch with your brother yet?"

Morgan started to clear the table when she was suddenly pulled across Nick's lap. "No, I forgot. Let Mary do that. I want to show you something." He picked her up and carried her to the living room with her legs wrapped around his hips. As the door swung shut behind them, he pressed her against the wall and his body.

"Morgan, let me taste you." He ran his tongue up her throat and along her jaw to her mouth. As soon as his mouth covered hers, she moaned. The feel of his body pressed to her, his mouth doing wonderful things, made her forget that she was supposed to avoid him. When his hand gently cupped her breast through his shirt, she nearly cried out; the sensations ripping through her body nearly had her begging for more.

"Please, Nickolas, please." She was begging, begging for him to do what, she didn't know, but her need for him was overwhelming.

"I wish I could take you. Take you right here, right now, but we can't. Not now. The babies…we can't have sex because of the babies."

The babies. Oh, God, the babies. What was she thinking? Of course he didn't want to have sex with her; she was huge. Not particularly sexy-looking either. She tried to pull away from him, but he held her fast.

"Morgan, look at me. Morgan!"

She was so ashamed she could only look at the wall over his shoulder.

"Morgan, it's not you. Please, look at me."

"I'm sorry. I want you to let me go. I'm so... large. Please let me down." It wasn't until he pulled her chin to him that she looked at him.

"I want you. I've never wanted to be buried so deep inside of a woman in all my life. I want to feel you come around me, over me. I want to feel your body milk mine until I'm so crazed with need that I can't see straight, but we can't. You can't have sex anymore once you lose your plug. It's no longer safe for the babies. But that doesn't mean we can't give each other pleasure. I want to see you come Morgan, taste you when you do."

Morgan realized that he had taken them to his bedroom again when he slid her down his body. She could feel his cock pressing hard against her belly. Need, the need to feel him inside of her raced through her. Nick gently pressed her back against his bed all the while kissing her, touching her.

Nick had his shirt unbuttoned from her before she realized it and her bra pushed down over her engorged breast. They had been so tender lately that she could barely stand to wash them. But what he was doing was sensual and gentle.

"Morgan, watch me suckle at your breast. I want to see your eyes glaze when you start to come. Watch me, baby."

Morgan leaned up and watched as he traced his tongue all along the areola, never touching the sensitive tip. His eyes never leaving hers, he flicked his tongue quickly over her nipple once, twice more before he covered it with his hot mouth and sucked.

Morgan cried out from the feel of him rolling her nipple on his tongue and against the roof of the hot cavern. She felt him shift and then his hand was touching her between her legs through the material of her panties. She couldn't decide which felt better, his hand or his lips, and soon it didn't matter. Her entire body was a live wire, waiting, waiting and wanting something.

"Please, I need...please help me, Nickolas." She nearly cried out again when he pulled his head away from her breast. He could be stopping. *Please*, she silently begged him, *don't stop.*

Nick moved down her body and off the bed. It didn't take her long to figure out where he was going and what he was going to do. Before she could protest and tell him to stop, he had his mouth covering her clit and she came apart, shattering into a million stars in the dark sky.

As he stood, she sat up and reached for him. She wanted to taste him as he had her. Fumbling with his buckle, she touched him as soon as he was free. His cock was hard and hot in her hands as she guided him to her mouth. Licking the tiny drop at the end of his shaft, she moaned at the taste. He was hot and spicy, hard and smooth.

Opening her mouth around him, he surged forward and bumped the back of her throat, causing her to gag slightly. He pulled back, cupped the back of her head, and gently showed her how to take him. Wrapping her hand around the inches she couldn't take in her mouth, she slid her hand up and down him.

"Morgan, please...I'm so close, baby. I'm going to come."

And she felt the first hot splash of him down the back of her throat. He rocked harder and harder as he came. Reaching between her own legs still spread wide from him, she touched herself and came with him, moaning around his cock.

Morgan fell back against the bed, spent as he slowly crawled along her and to her side. She felt euphoric and happy. She laid her head on his chest and listened as his heart slowed. Her mind was all fuddled and still fuzzy from what they'd done.

"I love you, Nickolas. I think I always have." She felt him stiffen beneath her. It was slight, but the way they were laying made it impossible for her not to feel it. Flushing with heat, she sat up, pulling away from him.

"Morgan, I'm sorry. I just can't... I don't know how I feel about you. I like you, but love... I don't know. I..."

Morgan cut him off before he said anything else. What he'd said already was enough. "I'm sorry. I should go. I have things to do today and I need to..."

Morgan buttoned up his shirt and moved quickly toward his door. He hadn't moved off the bed. As she made her way into the living room, she heard him call out to her. Blinded by her tears, she didn't stop, but grabbed up her bag that luckily was lying by the open elevator doors. The doors were nearly shut when he stepped out of the bedroom, and snapped closed as he got to them.

Morgan pushed buttons on the panel at random, hoping that she could stop it before she got to the lowest level. She had no doubt that someone would try and stop her if she went out the lobby.

The elevator stopped on the tenth floor, and she stepped off. As she did, she heard the bell ringing on the phone. No way was she answering it. Moving quickly toward the stairs, she opened the door and started down. She didn't know where she was going, but down seemed her best bet for getting out.

By the time she made it to the fifth level, she knew she was in trouble. The third floor was a blur of pain and dizziness. When she stopped on the main level, she was bleeding, badly.

Pushing through the doors to the main lobby, someone was screaming. Over and over they screamed until she just wanted them to shut up. Blurry things were moving in and out of her vision; she could hear voices, but couldn't make out what was being said. She felt someone try to lift her, but the person started screaming again. And she was put back down. Morgan could feel the darkness pulling at her now, starting to climb its way up her arms to her head. She saw him then, saw the phantom Nickolas. Before the blackness took her, he needed to know something. He needed to know what he'd done to her.

"I hate you. I want you to go away and never come near me again," she said to the dream just before the darkness took her.

CHAPTER FORTY-TWO

Nick had been sitting by Morgan's bed for the past two days. He'd only left the hospital once and that was because his mother had threatened to have Damon sedate him if he didn't leave for at least an hour. So he did, and was back in exactly sixty minutes.

"Nicky, any word yet?" Devin had been in and out a lot. He'd been bringing him food and drinks. He hadn't eaten anything, but Devin continued to bring them.

"No, she's still out. Damon said that she's healthy and strong and the babies are doing well so we shouldn't worry." Sure, he thought. Not to worry. She'd almost killed herself getting away from him.

They were both quiet for a few minutes before Nick spoke again. "I couldn't tell her I loved her. She ran from me—no, I drove her away because I couldn't say I love her."

"Do you? Love her, I mean?"

That was all he'd thought about since he'd seen her lying there bleeding on the cold floor in his lobby. And her screams; he could still hear them, echoing through his head and tearing into his heart like a blade. But it was her words, her telling him that she hated him that hurt the most. It was right then that he knew what his heart had been trying to tell him all along. He loved Morgan Becky Grant. He thought he'd been in love with her from the very first time that he'd met her only he'd been too stubborn and much too stupid to realize what a wonderful and giving woman she was.

"Yes. Yes, I love her. There is so much about her that I...she makes me laugh. I have never laughed so much until I met her. Did you know that she has her own business? I've never met a braver person than Morgan. I don't think she'll ever believe me. But I do. Oh God, Devin, I've fucked this up so badly." He leaned forward in his chair and rested his head on his hands.

Nick looked up at her as she moaned. She didn't move so once every shift, one of the nurses would come in and roll her to her side, one side then the other. They were doing it for the babies' sake. Her lying on the bed like that gave them less room to move and they needed to get into a better position to be born.

It wouldn't be long now, Damon told him. Morgan would need to stay on complete bed rest for at least another week before he felt better about letting her go into labor again. She had been in the beginning stages of it when she'd been brought in. They'd stopped it with drugs. The loss of blood and the ten flights of stairs had weakened her and he feared for her health if they didn't wait. But, he told him, she would need to be awake before he'd start her labor up.

That had been two days ago. He stood up, walked over to her bed, and looked down at her. Her skin was warmer than it had been in the ambulance. Her lips were still slightly blue, but not like they had been. Nick felt for her pulse and was relieved that it felt strong against his fingers.

"Oh, Morgan, I'm so very sorry for everything I've done to you. I want you to wake up and scream and yell at me. Give me that look, the one that says 'you are just too stupid, aren't you?' Come on, Morgan, please wake up." He sat down again, closer to the bed, and laid his head on her and cried.

~~~

Morgan blinked open her eyes against the harsh light. She didn't know where it was coming from, but it seemed to be shining right into her head.

"Hello, Morgan. Welcome back." It was Damon and he was the source of light. He was trying to blind her with a flashlight that she could finally see in his hand. He let her move away from the light.

"Where...where am?" She couldn't make her words form, but he seemed to understand.

"You're in Grant Hospital. You've been here four days. You gave us quite a scare. Please don't do that again. Do you remember what happened?"

Nickolas. She'd been at Nickolas' apartment. Sex. She'd told him... Yes, it came back to her with perfect clarity. He'd said he didn't love her.

"Yes. When can I go home?" His laughter startled her. She wanted to go home. There were still things she needed to get taken care of.

"I believe it would be better if you stayed here. At least until the babies are born. You've been in and out of labor for the past four days. Now that you're awake, I'd like to deliver them and get them into your arms for a change. How does that sound?"

"Labor? I don't...it doesn't hurt. Shouldn't it hurt?" She rubbed her hand along her belly and felt the difference immediately. It was harder and lower.

"You will. I need to call Nicky and let him know..."

"*No!* I don't want him here. I don't want to see him. He'll... when they're born, then he can come. Not yet."

"I'm sorry, Morgan, but I have to call him. He's my brother

and I can't... Whatever differences you two have can be worked out, but he'll never get this opportunity again to see his first child born."

Morgan knew he was right. And, she thought, its part of the contract they had together, that he be there when they were born. She only nodded and turned away from him. She didn't know how long labor was, but it would be over soon and she'd be moving on.

Nickolas arrived an hour later. Damon told her that he waited as long as he could, telling her she needed to be prepped anyway.

Morgan was taken down to labor and delivery about twenty minutes after she woke up. She already had an IV in, so all they needed to do was add another line to the one she already had running. Damon explained all the equipment to her and what he was going to use to begin with. She had opted for an epidural and they were waiting until she was five centimeters before they administered it to her. Damon had just finished examining her when Nickolas walked in.

"Good timing. She's moving right along now. You're at four centimeters now, so within the next hour, we'll have Dick come in and give you some happy meds. You'll need to be very still when he injects you so you'll need someone to hold you. Nicky, can you hold her up while he does it?"

"No, he doesn't have to. I'd rather...it's okay. I don't need him to hold me. I'll be very still," she said.

"Morgan, don't be stupid. He'll hold you. Now, I don't want any more of this shit going on in my delivery room, understand me? The two of you will work together on this, or I'll go home. I've got more important things to do than to watch you two bicker about who does what. I'm in charge, and do as I say." Damon looked at her first and when she nodded, he glared at his brother.

When he nodded too, Damon started barking orders to the staff.

"Mom and the others are in the waiting room. They want to know if it's okay if they come in to see you before we start."

Morgan realized that this would be the last time she'd see them. Because after today, there'd be no reason for them to want her around anymore. She nodded at him, her throat suddenly closed up tight.

Mrs. Parker came in first, and hugged her tightly. Morgan took her hand and laid it on the foot she could feel pressing tightly against her belly.

"Thank you, Mrs. Parker. Thank you for everything you did for me," Morgan said to her softly.

"Morgan, do you think you could call me Margaret just this once? I was hoping for Mom, but I'll take Margaret."

"Thank you, Margaret. Thank you very much." With another tight hug, she left. The men came in next. All five of them huddled around her like a brigade of troops.

They all hugged her tightly and Spencer handed her a small planter from Meggie. "They won't let her come up. But Tansy said she'd sneak her up later to see you." Morgan nodded. She was beginning to think that she'd never be able to speak again around the knot in her throat. A few minutes later, they were ushered out.

Dick Sergeant came in and told her what was involved in the epidural. She leaned all her weight forward onto Nick so that Dr. Sergeant could get her back without any problems.

The pain was horrific and she couldn't hold back her cry no matter how hard she tried. Nick started cooing at her, telling her he had her. She couldn't listen over the pain. Soon, it was over and she was lying back on the bed.

Almost at once, she could feel the pain recede. She knew the contractions were getting stronger because the monitor on the wall would beep rapidly when she had one. Nick had started telling her when the contractions were beginning, but she wouldn't look at him, so he stopped.

At six-thirty, nearly five hours after she was injected, she felt the urge to push. The room became a blur of movements and voices. Nick kept mopping her face and giving her ice chips whenever she seemed to need them. They had long given up even the pretense of trying to talk to one another. He just watched her, and when she must have looked needy, he'd mop.

"All right, Morgan, Nicky, it's show time. You're fully dilated and effaced. The next time you have the urge to push, Morgan, I want you to push from here, all right?" He patted her bottom as he spoke.

Nick was asked to get up behind her on the bed and hold her up, bending her at the waist to help with the pushing. He was to keep her focused and to have her rest between contractions. Without a word, he did what he was asked.

Nearly thirty minutes later, Damon shouted he had a head. Five minutes after that, he was laying a little body on her lap. Morgan closed her eyes. She couldn't get attached to him this late in the game. When the nurse took him away, she leaned heavily back against Nick before she thought. She started to pull away and forward when he told her to be still.

"Did you see our son, Morgan? Isn't he beautiful?"

She didn't answer because the next contraction hit hard.

Baby boy two didn't want to be born, she thought. Not that she could blame him. The world was cold and cruel. Twenty-nine minutes after his brother came into the world, baby boy Grant two was born.

Morgan was drained and exhausted. By time they had

finished cleaning her up and her bed cleaned too, she was asleep. She didn't move when they came into check her, nor did she stir when someone came in and took her temperature and blood pressure. For a full twenty-eight hours, she slept.

CHAPTER FORTY-THREE

As soon as she opened her eyes, she searched for the phone. It was time to go. Morgan knew that the sooner she left, the better off everyone would be. She reached for the phone to call Mrs. Sugar.

By prior arrangement, Libby would come as soon as she called her. Libby would come to the hospital and bring Morgan everything she needed to leave and while she left the hospital, Libby would wait in her bed until some noticed the switch. Morgan wasn't waiting to be released. She was just going to go.

"I'm ready, can you come now?" Morgan didn't even know what time is was and hoped that she hadn't woke them up. Mick sounded fine and wide awake when he answered.

"Yeah, darling. We'll be there as soon as I can get the car started. Should be in about ten minutes."

They were there in seven. Morgan moved to the bathroom and changed with Libby's help. She hadn't realized she'd be so weak. Only having to stop twice, she was dressed in less than five minutes. She was nearly to the door when she turned around and put the little planter that Meggie had sent her into her regular purse.

Morgan was leaving the pink bag behind. There was no way she could carry it without someone noticing it. Also, she didn't know if she could look at it again without thinking of all that she was leaving behind. Kissing Libby on the cheek, Morgan and Mick left her room. She was crying softly when they got to the elevators and nearly had to be carried by Mick by the time they got there.

Mick pushed the button for the elevator and looked at her. "Morgan, honey, I want you to know that we love you like a daughter. In fact, sometimes, I think we love you more than our own kids. I want you to know this was the hardest thing I've ever done."

"Thank you, Mr. Mick. I'll always remember this. I swear I'll try and keep in touch with you." The elevator dinged and she looked at it expectantly.

"I surely hope so. Morgan, I'm so sorry honey. But this is the only way. It had to be done." She looked at him, confused, and watched as he walked away. As the door opened, she suddenly understood.

"Morgan, love, were you going somewhere?"

Damn it. Mick had ratted her out to Nickolas.

"Dr. Grant. I'm going home. We had a deal. I lived up to my part, now I want you to live up to yours. Let me go home." If she didn't sit down soon, she was going to fall down. Damn him for being a strong man.

"I want to show you something first. It's just down here." He stepped out of the elevator and took her arm and headed them toward the nursery. Not now; she couldn't do this now.

"Oh no, I don't think so. The last time you wanted to 'show' me something, I made a fool of myself. If it's all the same to you, I'll just stay right here and you can show someone else. Someone more in your league." Okay, the wall was looking really good right now. Moving toward it, because the stupid thing was moving, she reached out to touch it. It suddenly wasn't there. It had moved at least ten more feet away.

That stupid floor was moving now, so fast too. If she wanted to, she thought, she could practically touch it without bending over. But the shouting, it had to go. "Morgan? Morgan!"

~~~

Slowly, Morgan started to make her way up from the deep darkness where she'd been. She felt heavy and weightless at the same time. She opened her eyes and looked around in the semi darkness. The hospital again. Damn it, was she never going to be able to make a clean escape.

"No, I don't plan on letting you escape again," Nickolas said from behind her. She rolled over to her back and looked toward where she thought he was. He was lying in the bed next to her.

"I thought I was talking to myself. I didn't realize that I'd spoken out loud. Why are you here? I thought you'd be home with your sons."

Morgan wanted to reach up and smooth the hair off his forehead. Touching him would solve so many of life's problems, and create so many more.

"I can't take them yet. I haven't even been down to see them yet," he said softly.

How was that possible? She'd been here at least two days. Damon said that they were healthy and...oh God!

"What's happened to them, Nickolas? Are they hurt? Sick? Tell me. Oh, my poor little... Why are you laughing at me? This is not funny." She smacked him on the chest.

"You know, you only call me by my first name when you're being passionate about something? Our sons are fine. I wanted to see them the first time with their mom. You see, I got this delivered the morning before you had them." He leaned over and picked up something from the bedside table. "In it is the deed to the house and an account that gives them all your money. I thought that was a very strange gesture for a woman who claims she doesn't know how to love anyone."

"I loved you and look where that got me." She regretted it as soon as she said it. "I'm sorry. I shouldn't...it's not your fault. I'm just, I'd like for you to go now." Morgan tried to roll back over and he stopped her.

"Morgan, I'm the one who is sorry. I was stupid and..." He paused and looked down at her.

"Yeah, go on."

He burst out laughing. Then she did something incredibly stupid. She let him kiss her.

It was tender and soft. Barely a touch to her mouth. His breath was warm, his tongue hot against her lips. When he pulled her lower lip into his mouth, she moaned at the sensations he created.

"Oh, Morgan. I do love you."

Pulling back from him, she looked at his face. Tears had welled in his eyes and he looked so sad.

"I have to tell you a story. My wife Margo and I had been childhood sweethearts. I met her in first grade and we stayed as friends, even when I went to private school. We didn't always get along. Seldom a day went by that we didn't fight about something. As we got older, the fights took on a surreal quality to them. We'd fight then have this incredible sex. But now I realize that's all it was. Sex.

"When I got out of high school and moved home, she was there. One night after we'd had sex, she told me she was pregnant. I was overwhelmed and happy. A baby. Of course, we got married a few weeks later, and that's when things started getting bad.

"You see, she wasn't pregnant at all. She'd trapped me. About a month after our wedding, she started having an affair. I guess I knew she'd been sleeping around, but I thought after we married she'd settle down. It only got worse." He rolled to his back and pulled her to him tightly. Morgan didn't say anything but let him talk.

"On our first wedding anniversary, she claims she's pregnant again."

He was quite for so long she thought he was going to stop. She knew that this is what he'd been leading up to. Leaning up, she looked down at him this time. "It wasn't yours, was it? Oh, Nickolas... she was a fucking bitch."

He laughed and pulled her to him again. "My protector. Yes, she was. She claimed the baby was mine. But I knew that we'd stopped having sex about three months before this. It wasn't as though she hadn't been trying to...hummm, lure me back, but I'd just had enough. Then when that wasn't working, a couple of months later, she said that it was my father's. I didn't want to believe her. I'm still not sure, but..."

"They died together. It wasn't your dad's either. I just know it. She wanted to hurt you and found a way to do it. Oh, Nickolas, I'm so sorry." She huddled down onto his chest again and cried softly over his heart.

"Morgan, I love you. I should have said that to you long before now. I should have said a lot of things to you long before now. I want you to come home with me, build a life with me, for me. I want you to help me raise our children. I want to have more babies with you."

"I don't know how to love anyone, and I've no clue about children. I don't know if I can do this."

"Morgan, you gave your entire savings, house, and everything you own to our sons. What does that say about you?"

"It says that I'm barely making a dent in what you have to give them. It's all I had, all I thought I could leave them."

"Yes, baby, it says you love them. No matter how hard you tried not to, you still fell in love with them. You were going to leave them a part of you, something of you, from you. That's love, and that's why I love you." He kissed her again. This time, it was with love. She could feel it.

"I'm going to go and have the nurse bring us our babies. Then Mom is going to bring us some dinner and we're going to have a huge family discussion." He hopped off the bed and was striding toward the door.

"Wait! What kind of family discussion? Nickolas, what are you talking about?"

"Why we have to name them, don't we?"

Morgan looked at him, really looked at him. Name them? She glared at him as he came back toward the bed.

"You've not named our sons? Right now they are laying down there in that nursery and people are calling them Grant boy one and Grant boy two. Oh Nickolas, how could you?" She was trying hard not to laugh; the expression on his face was priceless. "What do you think the other children are going to say to them? They will be teased and teased. Is that what you want?"

Nick put his fingers over his lips and seemed to contemplate her query. "Maybe they won't notice they don't have names. Maybe they'll be so overwhelmed with our combined beauty in them that the other children won't notice. I'll go get them and we'll make sure they aren't too scarred." His quick kiss had her reeling.

Morgan sat up a little more in the bed as soon as he left. She was sore and tired, but she was suddenly filled with...love, she realized. She was filled with love. When the door opened again, a nurse was pushing a large bassinet at her with Nickolas right behind her. Morgan couldn't help the happiness she felt at seeing her sons. Hers and Nickolas' sons.

When the nurse handed her the first little bundle, she didn't know what to do. Terror at hurting him, dropping him, nearly had her pull away. But the moment he was settled in her arms, it was as if she'd come home. And when Nickolas settled down next to her and was handed his blue bundle, everything came together. Family.

Morgan leaned back against her husband and held her little boy in her arms and knew what his name was. "This one is Anthony Patrick Grant and his little brother is Nickolas Markus Grant. They'll be called Anthony and Markus. What do you think?"

"I think, love, that is perfect. Absolutely perfect. I love you."

"I love you too, Nickolas, and I always will."

About the Author
Kathi S. Barton

I woke up one morning and decided to give play time to the people in my head who were keeping me awake. Little did I know that they would be so relentless and want their time right now! I wrote for the pure joy of it and to entertain my family and friends. But mostly it was to get more than an hour of sleep without a story playing out. Of course, the more I write, the more they want. So…well, as a result of sleepless days (I work through the night as a gun toting grandma – nope not a vigilantly but an armed security guard) I have lots of stories written.

Hello! My name is Kathi Barton and I'm an author. I have been married to my very best friend Sonny for at times seems several lifetimes – in a good way, honey. And together we have three wonderful children and then the ones we brought into the world - Paul and Dale Barton, Jason and Wendy Barton and Danielle and Ben Conklin. They have given us seven of the greatest treasures on Earth. They don't live at home seven days a week! No, seriously, seven grandchildren – Gavin, Spring, Ben, Trinity, Sarah, Kelly and Kian.

www.ingramcontent.com/pod-product-compliance
Lightning Source LLC
Chambersburg PA
CBHW020604180626
46810CB00007B/2638